Praise for Lexi Blake and Masters and Mercenaries...

"I can always trust Lexi Blake's Dominants to leave me breathless...and in love. If you want sensual, exciting BDSM wrapped in an awesome love story, then look for a Lexi Blake book."

~Cherise Sinclair USA Today Bestselling author

"Lexi Blake's MASTERS AND MERCENARIES series is beautifully written and deliciously hot. She's got a real way with both action and sex. I also love the way Blake writes her gorgeous Dom heroes--they make me want to do bad, bad things. Her heroines are intelligent and gutsy ladies whose taste for submission definitely does not make them dish rags. Can't wait for the next book!"

~Angela Knight, New York Times bestselling author

"A Dom is Forever is action packed, both in the bedroom and out. Expect agents, spies, guns, killing and lots of kink as Liam goes after the mysterious Mr. Black and finds his past and his future... The action and espionage keep this story moving along quickly while the sex and kink provides a totally different type of interest. Everything is very well balanced and flows together wonderfully."

~A Night Owl "Top Pick", Terri, Night Owl Erotica

"A Dom Is Forever is everything that is good in erotic romance. The story was fast-paced and suspenseful, the characters were flawed but made me root for them every step of the way, and the hotness factor was off the charts mostly due to a bad boy Dom with a penchant for dirty talk."

~Rho, The Romance Reviews

"A good read that kept me on my toes, guessing until the big reveal, and thinking survival skills should be a must for all men."

~Chris, Night Owl Reviews

Cherished

Other Books by Lexi Blake

EROTIC ROMANCE

Masters And Mercenaries
The Dom Who Loved Me
The Men With The Golden Cuffs
A Dom Is Forever
On Her Master's Secret Service
Sanctum: A Masters and Mercenaries Novella
Love and Let Die
Unconditional: A Masters and Mercenaries Novella
Dungeon Royale
Dungeon Games: A Masters and Mercenaries Novella
A View to a Thrill
Cherished: A Masters and Mercenaries Novella
You Only Love Twice, *Coming February 17, 2015*
Adored: A Masters and Mercenaries Novella, *Coming May 12, 2015*

Masters Of Ménage (by Shayla Black and Lexi Blake)
Their Virgin Captive
Their Virgin's Secret
Their Virgin Concubine
Their Virgin Princess
Their Virgin Hostage
Their Virgin Secretary
Their Virgin Mistress, *Coming April 14, 2015*

CONTEMPORARY WESTERN ROMANCE

Wild Western Nights
Leaving Camelot, Coming Soon

URBAN FANTASY

Thieves
Steal the Light
Steal the Day
Steal the Moon
Steal the Sun
Steal the Night
Ripper, A Thieves Novel, *Coming January 20, 2015*

Cherished
A Masters and Mercenaries Novella

Masters and Mercenaries, Book 7.5

Lexi Blake

Cherished: A Masters and Mercenaries Novella
Masters and Mercenaries, Book 7.5
Lexi Blake

Published by DLZ Entertainment LLC

Copyright 2014 DLZ Entertainment LLC
Edited by Chloe Vale
Print ISBN: 978-1-937608-39-2

McKay-Taggart logo design by Charity Hendry

Sign up for Lexi Blake's newsletter
and be entered to win a $25 gift certificate
to the bookseller of your choice.

Join us for news, fun, and exclusive content
including free short stories.

There's a new contest every month!

Go to http://www.lexiblake.net/contact.html to
subscribe.

Acknowledgements

Special thanks to my team—Chloe Vale, Riane Holt, and Stormy Pate. Thanks to Charity Hendry for the beautiful graphics. As always, thanks to Rich and my amazing family for all their support.

This book is for Lee, who carries a piece of my heart with him always.

Chapter One

There was something deeply humiliating about begging and pleading while wearing a corset and a thong. Oh, Bridget Slaten was fairly certain it helped most women get what they wanted, but it didn't seem to be working for her. Then again, she was kind of using the tools on the wrong crowd. Somehow, she didn't see her gay hubby and female and straight best friend responding to her boobs hanging out.

She looked across the room and saw Will Daley striding across the club toward the bar. Would he respond to her boobs hanging out?

She consigned that line of thinking to the same place she always shoved the idea of writing that science fiction romance where her heroine was the only woman left on an earth made up entirely of Channing Tatums. Sure it was a fun idea, but it wouldn't work in the long run. The man made her heart pound—Will in this case, though obviously Channing did it for her, too—but there was zero chance that she would have anything to do with either of them. Will was out of her league looks wise and she wasn't looking for a one-night hookup, which was all a woman ever got from him.

No way. No how. She'd gone through too much crap to willingly walk into the fire again. She hadn't had sex since she'd kicked Benjy out, and that was probably the safest bet.

Still, she couldn't help but watch the way he moved, his every limb a testament to masculine grace.

"If you don't watch out you're going to need a rag to catch the drool, honey," Chris said.

She turned to one of her two best friends. Both Chris Roberts and Serena Dean-Miles were sitting in the decadent booth where their Doms had left them. Bridget sighed because no one had ordered her to wait for him. She'd only been coming to Sanctum for three weeks. She couldn't expect that she would find a regular in that time. She wasn't stupid. She knew she was considered a bit difficult. She'd been training with two of the approved regulars, Jesse Murdoch, who was a sweetheart and a half, and Mitchell Bradford, who kind of scared the crap out of her, but he was good with ropes. Still, they weren't hers and never would be. She was, as she always seemed to be, alone among the happily paired off. Time. It simply took time. That's what she tried to tell herself. Some day her Dom would come and all that shit.

She knew one thing though. It wouldn't be gorgeous, smart, hunky, hot and manwhorey neurosurgeon Dr. William Daley.

"I am not drooling. It's just weird to see him here. He moved into my building last month." She'd watched him moving his boxes in, the Texas heat causing him to sweat and get rid of that shirt he should never, ever be allowed to wear. His chest was a work of art, and he had those notches on his hips she wrote about so lovingly in her romance novels. She'd stared at him and sighed, and he'd looked up at her with an arrogant grin right before three women walked up behind him, obviously helping him move. A harem. He had a harem of beautiful women who followed him around. They came to his condo at all hours of the day or night, sometimes in singles, more often as a slender, graceful pack.

She'd already been one of many and she hadn't even known about it until the end. She wasn't going to walk into a relationship where the man was sure to cheat.

"It's all my fault. Well, not really mine. It's Derek's. I told him about the empty condos and he's been mentoring Will. When Will changed jobs, he wanted a new place because of…well, because of the stuff that went down." Serena's voice trailed off.

Stuff? There was stuff? Shit. She really wanted to know the stuff. Like now, but she forced herself to play it cool. She kept staring straight ahead and kept her tone as negligent as possible. "Stuff?"

Chris snorted, a sound he somehow managed to make elegant. "Don't even try it, sweetie. You can't make me believe you aren't interested in that man."

Serena bit her bottom lip and sighed—a sure sign that she knew something everyone else didn't. She'd been best friends with Serena and Chris for a very long time, and she knew their tells. And naturally they knew hers. "I don't know that being interested in Master Will is a good idea. Why don't you let me set you up with one of the new guys? There are some seriously cute men Ian's recruiting lately."

She'd seen them. She liked to call them baby Doms. From what she understood, they were almost all ex-military, and every damn one of them was seeing Sanctum's brand new resident shrink. Since Eve and Alex were on the cusp of adopting, Eve had pulled back and so Ryan, Sanctum's manager, and Ian Taggart, the owner of the club, had decided to hire a shrink—Kai Ferguson. He'd seemed to be some hippy dippy pretty boy until the first time she'd seen him wield a whip. Kai had approved her application but not before explaining that she had daddy issues and abandonment issues that she should really deal with.

Yeah, like she didn't know about those. In fact, those were exactly the issues she needed to deal with tonight. She tended to like to forget about her horrible, awful, very nasty parents, but her sister had made it so she couldn't avoid them. Whatever secrets hottie Will was hiding would have to wait.

"I need a date to my sister's wedding."

Both heads turned.

"What?" Serena asked.

"I thought you weren't going." Chris shook his head as if to say that was a bad idea.

She fricking knew it was a bad idea, but she was trapped. Of her entire family, she only still talked to her sister, Amy, on a regular basis. Amy, who she'd protected as a kid. Amy, who had begged her to come to the wedding and then screwed her over.

She couldn't leave Amy alone amongst the barbarian horde. She wished Amy had left her some dignity. "She's my sister. She called me. I have to go. Besides, I should meet whatever douchebag my dad picked for her so I know who I need to kill later in life."

Serena leaned forward. "Maybe Amy's in love."

"Maybe Daddy's in debt." Somehow she seriously doubted that Amy had magically fallen in love with the exact person who could boost her father's company and who happened to want to get married at the exact right time. "Look, I know my father. He tried to pull the same shit with me. How do you think I got kicked out and disinherited? I wouldn't marry the man he wanted me to. Larry Halford of Halford Properties. Dear old dad wanted to expand and he views his daughters as assets to be given away at his behest. He was born about a thousand years too late. He would have made a great feudal lord, and by great I really mean awful and unfair."

"Sheeeit," Chris said in a slow Texas drawl. "Well, I'm glad you're going. She asked me weeks ago and I hated the idea of going without you. I wasn't going to tell you because I know how you feel about it."

Amy had met Chris and Serena several times. It didn't surprise Bridget that Amy had invited her friends. And it made what she was going to ask a little simpler. "So which hot hubby are you taking, Serena? Because I really need to borrow the other one. Amy fucked up and told everyone I'm flipping engaged."

Serena's eyes widened. "Are you serious? Why would she do that?"

Bridget sighed. "She was at one of her many showers and the cousins started talking shit about me and how I can't find a man to save my life because I'm fat—very original—and no man wants a woman who writes smut. No good man that is. The family has a problem with the way I make a living. Amy was the slightest bit tipsy and said I wasn't only seeing someone, I'm freaking engaged, so now to avoid both my humiliation and hers, I need a fiancé. I'm thinking Adam. He's perfect and he doesn't scare me the way Jake does."

Serena's head shook. "Jake is a sweetheart. He isn't scary."

Jacob Dean was former military and unlike his brethren, Kai, he didn't need to wear leathers and wield a whip for everyone in the vicinity to know that he was a predator. With a body to die for and a face that could have been hewn from granite, Jake Dean looked like a man who had once been a Green Beret and now served as muscle for one of the world's premier security agencies.

He would be at the wedding in a work capacity since McKay-Taggart provided security for her father's corporation, but maybe she could pass off Adam Miles as her boy toy.

Adam was a gorgeous piece of metro hotness. He was always perfectly dressed, always lovingly groomed, and the man knew how to take care of a woman. While Jake handled all of the heavy stuff, Adam was the day-to-day man. He took care of Serena's schedule and made sure she didn't forget to eat. He made sure she came back to earth after spending the day in her head making up stories. Both of Serena's men adored her and they were both great fathers to their son, Tristan. Was it too much to ask that she kind of, sort of borrowed one for her sister's wedding?

"I know Jake's a great guy, but I think my dad's met him so I need Adam to play my fiancé for the week."

Serena looked at her like she'd grown two heads. "I'm not letting you borrow one of my husbands, Bridge. I love you, but they would protest. We're going to Hawaii. I had to convince the guys to let me come, and do you know how I managed that? By offering them sex. Both of them."

They could have all the tropical sex they wanted as long as they didn't do it in front of the wedding party. "Well, I didn't plan on sleeping with him. Come on." She pulled out the big guns. She touched her side. "Sorry. It's a bit of pain from where I lost my spleen."

Serena went a little white. Serena always did when reminded of the day she'd almost been murdered by her vicious ex-husband and the husband of her and Bridget and Chris's literary agent, who took extreme exception to his wife representing "smutty" authors. Douchewad. Bridget was happy they were all dead. Except Lara. She still missed Lara. Her new agent was a lesbian whose partner was a big fan, so that was a plus. Losing her spleen because she'd gotten in the way of all the murders had been kind of crappy, but it had caused her to reevaluate her life and it did give her a go-to when she needed some guilt to back her up.

"I'll talk to him," Serena said.

Chris put a hand out. "No, you won't." He pointed that terrifically judgmental right index finger of his Bridget's way. "I told you the last time was the last time."

"But all I got out of it was the last Diet Coke in the fridge," she complained.

"I believe I pointed that out at the time. It's been over a year. The spleen is now off the table and you can't use it," Chris pronounced. "Serena, you're officially off the hook for something you didn't actually do in the first place."

"It seems wrong to have traded my spleen for a Diet Coke," Bridget grumbled although she knew she would happily do it on her worst days. She needed the caffeine. Still, it probably was wrong of her. "Fine. Let's bargain. I'll let you have the next two hero names we argue over."

They tried not to have the same names in their books to avoid confusion, but when one wrote ménage, hero names became difficult to come by. She swore her next set of ménage boys would be named Fred, Maurice, and Algernon. That was all she was going to be left with. It was a good trade.

Serena's eyes narrowed. Yes, there was some interest there.

"It's not going to work and you can't trade your husband for use of the name Cash in your next book," Chris argued.

Oooo, she hadn't thought of that one.

"Dibs," she and Serena exclaimed at the same time.

Chris's eyes rolled. "Seriously? That was a joke name. And I don't think your family is going to buy Adam as your loving fiancé if he's sleeping in Serena's room."

Minor issues. "He can sneak out of my room at night."

"We're taking the baby with us," Serena explained. "I need both of them. Tristan is a handful. He doesn't like to sleep. Like ever."

"Okay, we can say that Adam's your manny." She could write a backstory. After all, she was a novelist. She could craft a whole fictional story to obfuscate the truth that she was kind of sad and alone. "That's how we met. I like that a lot. It's a meet-cute story. I fell for him because of his amazing diapering technique."

"Do you even hear your own cray cray anymore?" Chris asked, shaking his head.

"Adam isn't going to Hawaii as the manny, Bridget," a masculine voice said.

Damn it. She turned and Jake was frowning down at her. Yep. He scared her. She tried to give him a grin. "Come on, Jake."

Jake wasn't buying it. "Nope. There are now a bunch of unattached Doms at Sanctum. I'm pretty sure Ian imported them from Special Forces land. Oh and the doc and the lawyer. Pick from them. Any of them will do, but there's no way you're getting the dude who changes half the diapers. It's not happening. Also, your father's met Adam. He's our client, though you should know we both think your dad's a complete asshole but he pays his bills on time."

Well, his PA, who he was very likely sleeping with him, paid his bills on time. Perfect.

Serena sent her a sympathetic look. "You know who you want to ask."

Doctor Will, with the perfect pecs and biceps that she wanted to lick. "Yes. I wanted to ask Chris, but he's already met two of my cousins and insulted their taste in shoes because they're awful. They know we're never, ever going to sleep together. So I'm screwed. Maybe I can tell everyone I'm a lesbian. I could hire a hooker."

She could also interview the hooker and get some research out of this cluster fuck. Maybe that wasn't such a bad idea…

"Because that's not going to take away from your sister's wedding or anything." Serena shook her head. "You could tell everyone Amy was mistaken."

Another way to derail her sister's wedding. Her family was a cesspit of gossip and judgment. There was one way and only one way out, and that was to find someone to go with her, and her father would probably recognize a hooker from a hundred yards away. He was an expert, after all.

"Okay. It can't be too hard, right? I'm offering a free trip to Kauai. My father's sending a jet and paying for the ridiculous suite. All I have to do is take his intolerance, bigotry, and hatred, and I will be greeted with a gift basket on arrival. Wouldn't any man want a piece of that?"

Of course, taking a neurosurgeon would solve everything, including her desperate lust for one particular doctor.

She looked around but Will was nowhere to be found. Damn it.

She couldn't. It would be stupid, and the truth was it wasn't like she was his type. She'd seen the subs he preferred to work with. Thin. Deeply submissive. Not the "just for fun" girls. He would hear her bratty mouth go off and run the other way. She was sure the first time she flipped someone off on the road he would dump her. That was if and only if he would go out with her in the first place, which wasn't going to happen since he already had a trio of gorgeous women to choose from and his pick of the subs at Sanctum.

"You could ask one of the new guys," Chris offered. "Unless you want to ask Jesse. You've worked with him a couple of times."

She couldn't not notice the use of the word "work." Most people in

17

the lifestyle would have used the word "play." But she didn't play. She "worked." She used the time they gave her at Sanctum to research, never for herself but rather for the characters in her books. When she sat and interviewed the Doms who would talk to her, like Jesse and Alex McKay and Mitchell, she wasn't looking for someone for herself. She was merely thinking in terms of backstories and characters and good scenes.

Will Daley made her think of what it would be like to have her own Dom.

And that was precisely why she was going to stay away.

Decision made. "All right then. I think I'll talk to some of the baby Doms since Serena is so very selfish and you are incapable of looking like you want to sleep with me."

Serena pouted a little. "It's not selfishness."

She let her friend off the hook and leaned in for a hug. "I'm teasing you. I honestly couldn't handle Adam anyway. We would fight over the mirror."

Jake laughed and started teasing Serena about how Adam sometimes used her hair products. Chris's Dom returned and settled him on his lap.

Happy couples. Yep. They were all around her. Well, couples and trios. She noted Karina Mills walking into the bar holding hands with her fiancé, Derek Brighton.

So much happiness and not a bit of it seemed to be slated for her.

Great, now she was holding a pity party. Lovely.

She looked around. Beautiful men were everywhere. Even the ones who weren't conventionally attractive had character stamped on their faces. There was no doubt about it. It was a smorgasbord of male beauty.

Maybe it wouldn't be so bad to pretend to have a boyfriend for a while. Hell, maybe she'd even find someone she liked. Someone who wouldn't cheat on her and spend her money.

Or she could settle for not humiliating herself.

"Tomorrow. I'll make a list tonight and ask them tomorrow," she said more to herself than anyone else.

But her best friend was right there. Serena smiled and put a hand in hers. "I'll help you. Let's go get dressed and head back to our place for coffee."

"And baby watching," Bridget said quickly. Watching Tristan Miles-Dean had become her favorite pastime. She'd never really thought about babies until her best friend had one, and now she loved to look at the expressions he made while he was sleeping and the way he tried to eat his own foot.

Serena nodded. "And baby watching. We'll figure out the perfect guy to ask. It'll be fun."

Bridget doubted that it would be fun, but at least she wasn't alone. Chris gave her a wink.

No. She might not have a guy, but somehow she'd found the best friends a girl could ask for.

* * * *

"You're pathetic, you know." A sarcastic voice had Will Daley turning away from his current occupation of eavesdropper.

It didn't matter. It seemed the relevant conversation was over, so he flipped Mitchell Bradford off and slunk out from behind the sofa he'd been sitting on in time to watch Bridget Slaten saunter off in her heels and a miniskirt that left just the tiniest smidgen to his imagination. Fuck, that girl had the sweetest ass he'd seen in forever.

Unfortunately, it was attached to a banging body and the brattiest mouth he'd ever come across.

"I have to listen in because she won't talk to me." Will crossed his arms over his chest as she turned toward the locker room. He kept his voice down because Chris Roberts, his boyfriend and Dom Jeremy Hill, and Jake Dean were still talking.

Mitch shook his head. "I think that's what we call a signal in our world. You see, we're supposed to read body language and be able to tell when a sub is happy or distressed."

Will sighed and wished law school had made Mitch less sarcastic. "She's not unhappy. She's afraid of something."

Bridget Slaten was a complete mystery to him, and he wasn't exactly sure why, but he felt a desperate need to solve her. He'd first met her when Derek had found him a condo. Will figured Derek owed him since Derek and his fiancée, Karina, were the reason he'd nearly been murdered and humiliated horrifically, so when he decided on a fresh start and Derek offered, he'd taken them up on it.

Not at first. At first he had too much crap to deal with. There were police reports to be filed and explanations given of how a killer had almost gotten away with pinning his crimes on Will. There was Starr, who had used him for months when all she was really doing was getting close so her boyfriend could kill Karina and collect on an insurance policy. He could still see her, her normally placid face screwed up in disgust.

You're a pervert. The things you made me do. You're the one who should be going to jail. Not me.

He shook off that particular humiliation. He didn't like to think about the fact that her trial would be coming up soon.

It had been a motherfuck of a few months. Hence the need to start over.

And to shake off the past and embrace who he really was. He was a Dom and he needed this kind of play. He wasn't going to hide it anymore. He'd spent the last several years making sure no one at the hospital knew he liked to visit clubs. He'd gone so far as to live in Dallas and work in Fort Worth so he wouldn't run into anyone who knew him. He'd told lies about his profession.

He was still the kid who didn't want anyone to know he lived in a trailer and his mom was a meth head.

No. He didn't hide now and he wasn't going to hide his interest in Bridget. His sisters even teased him about her because he tended to trip or miss steps when she walked by.

"What makes you think she's afraid and not simply uninterested?" Mitch asked. There was no way Will could miss the speculative look in his friend's eyes. Mitch was a lawyer, a shark of the highest order. He was always assessing, always plotting.

Wishful thinking? "She watches me when she thinks I'm not looking."

Lila had been the one to inform him of that interesting nugget, though she was known for being ridiculously over positive at times. All three of his sisters tended to take a super-positive, the-world is-still-great view of life, which considering how they'd grown up was a miracle.

Mitch's big shoulder shrugged. "She could be worried you're stalking her. Which you are. I've found women have excellent prey instincts. They get antsy when the big bad predator keeps licking his chops around her."

"I'm not drooling over her, damn it." At least he hoped he wasn't. He had to admit he thought about those tits all the time. Real. Soft. Big. He was pretty sure he couldn't hold her breasts completely in the palm of his hand. They would overflow. She would never fit into the designer clothes the women at work dreamed about. She was too curvy, too womanly. Soft breasts flowed into curvy hips and that ass. "I'm interested. She's a gorgeous woman."

And now he understood that she was a woman with a problem. Yeah, his brain was chewing on that information. Aloha and all that.

"I didn't think she was your type."

"I have a type?"

Mitch rolled his dark eyes. "Dude, you've screwed every super sub here. You do know that she's only here for research, right? From what I understand, she's not looking for a Dom. I've worked with her a couple of times and she's very closed off. There's not a lot of trust there for anyone except her two sub friends. She wants to ask her questions and do some light impact play, but I don't think any of it really moves her. I've heard she writes romance books. What the hell does D/s have to do with fluffy romance books?"

Ah, the lawyer hadn't kept up with pop culture. "Didn't you know Doms are the new cowboys?" He'd heard Bridget and her friends laughing about some blog proclaiming that fact. They'd been of the firm opinion that cowboys were still cool. And Bridget had immediately started talking about a cowboy Dom as the coolest thing ever. "Bridget writes smutty books. Sex books. She's looking for new fetishes to write about. And she needs a Dom. There's a lost little sub under all that brattiness."

Not that he would be her Dom. No. He wasn't looking to be anyone's Dom. Not on a permanent basis. He simply wanted to play with her, spend some mutually pleasurable time inside that hot body of hers. Bridget wasn't the type of woman he would settle down with for more than a few nights. Weeks, maybe. A month tops.

They would kill each other—but they would likely be spectacular in bed, and damn, but he could use that.

"Smutty books?" Mitch huffed. "I don't see it. She's a romantic at heart. If she's writing books, I would bet my life they're about romantic fantasies."

Which only proved he hadn't spent a lot of time studying Bridget. Will had checked out her covers. They were super salacious, with naked bodies and titles like *Her Billionaire Masters*. Yep, in the plural. Somehow, he couldn't see that book being about love and commitment. No. Bridget had some interesting fantasies, and he was the man to make a couple of them come true.

Though not the ménage one. When he got in her bed—for however long he was there—he would be the only one there. He didn't share and he would make sure she understood that he could take care of her every need without a partner.

If he could only pin her down.

"She needs a date to her sister's wedding," he explained, his eyes on the locker room. He was waiting to see her one last time. He had it so damn bad.

"Interesting. I'm not sure how that will help you. If she's reluctant, I doubt that a couple of hours with bad champagne and a cover band are really going to help you plead your case."

He felt his lips curl up. The whole time she'd been talking, he'd had a scenario playing through his head. A scenario that ended with him on top of her. "Do you know who her father is?"

"Haven't had the pleasure."

Will doubted there was any pleasure involved. "George Slaten."

Mitchell whistled. "Are you telling me that Bratty Bridget is the heir to Slaten Industries?"

It had shocked the hell out of him, too. It was obvious she was doing well financially. She lived in a nice building in a good part of town. She drove a nice but not over-the-top car, but she'd come from a billion dollar world. Poor little rich girl. Will had known more than one of those, and it was one more reason to not be attracted to her.

His dick wasn't listening. His dick didn't care that she came from an overprivileged background. His dick didn't give a damn that she wasn't a woman who would bring him peace or even pretend to need him for anything but an orgasm. His dick just wanted her.

"Her sister is getting married and apparently it's a lavish event."

Mitchell nodded. "Big Tag recently signed Slaten Industries as a client. Adam's revamping their computer security."

"Apparently he and Jake are also working security for the week-long wedding festivities in Hawaii. And Bratty Bridget has been asked to bring a date."

A single brow rose over Mitch's eyes. "You think she's going to ask you?"

Not a chance in hell. "She's planning on sitting down with Serena to decide which of the Doms she's going to ask. They're going to make a list. I assure you, I won't be on it, but that's a mistake."

"You don't think the other guys would take care of her?"

"I think she'll walk all over the other guys. I think the other guys won't know what to do with her." He didn't know what to do with her, but he really wanted the chance to try.

"Maybe she'll ask me. We get along all right."

Wow. That was what red-hot rage felt like. It came out of nowhere and set his blood to boiling and his fists to clenching. The entire idea of Mitchell putting his hands on her body made him see red, and he knew damn well Mitch had already done it. Mitch had flogged her, but there hadn't been anything sexual about it. He'd watched them together, all the while thinking that there wasn't a spark between them. There had been no real connection, no flow of energy from Dom to sub, and yet he kind of wanted to take his friend apart for even suggesting that he be the one to go to Hawaii with her, to share a room with her, to pretend to be her lover.

Mitch held his hands up in obvious surrender. "All right. I'll say no if she asks. Will, you've got a serious problem. You look insane right now."

So he wasn't good at hiding his feelings. He sucked at it. He took a deep breath, schooling his expression. "Sorry. I would rather you didn't go out with Bridget."

"Yes, I can plainly see that you would rather kill me than let that happen." Mitch's expression turned thoughtful. "You only want to hook up with her, right?"

"Hook up" was a stupid term. He liked the old ways. "I wouldn't mind having a short-term affair. Nothing serious. Very casual."

Mitch's head nodded but in that way that let Will know he was indulging the crazy. "Yeah, I can see that."

"You're an asshole." He had also pretty much become Will's best friend. Over the weeks he'd been at Sanctum, he'd come to depend on Mitch, despite the fact that they had utterly different backgrounds. Mitch had proven to be the kind of man who didn't care that a person hadn't come from money. He respected the hell out of any man who could pull himself up. Will had been forced to pull his own ass up from the muck more than once, and he'd supported three sisters while he was doing it. Didn't the universe owe him a little pleasure? Didn't it owe him a couple of nights with the world's hottest brat? "I'm going to make sure she has nowhere else to go."

Mitch's lips curled up. "Really? You're going to talk to every Dom in the place and scare them off?"

He shrugged. "Scare them. Bribe them. Blackmail them. I don't care as long as she comes to me at the end of it."

"Well, you know I love a good takedown as much as the next guy. Try to make sure she doesn't get hurt. How can I help?"

She wouldn't get hurt. He knew the type. Bridget Slaten likely wasn't capable of really being hurt by someone like him. She would never see him as a suitable mate, so all he could ever tempt her into was an affair. Maybe even a D/s affair. The thought of dominating her made his dick jump. "Let's make a list of our own and start working our way through. By the time we're done, she'll know she has one option and one option only."

She caught his eye as she stepped out of the locker room now dressed in her usual armor of jeans and a black T-shirt and a pair of comfortable sandals. He'd noted that she never wore heels unless she was in the club. Her raven black hair flowed in tresses around her shoulders and he wondered what kind of shampoo she used and how it would feel to have all that hair spread out on his chest as he held her close.

She turned slightly and their eyes met, hers widening in a startled-doe look before turning distinctly arrogant and bratty as she turned her nose up and walked away.

Yeah, she was aware of him. And soon she would realize there was no escape.

Chapter Two

B ridget took a deep breath as she contemplated the hallway in front of her. She would have to walk by his place, and it looked like he'd left his door open. On this floor there were only four units, but naturally he'd taken the one right across from hers. Normally she could sneak in or out without ever seeing him because he kept weird hours. He was a whiz-kid surgeon, so he got called in at all hours of the day or night. She often wondered if the harem got bored when he worked long hours.

She couldn't do it. She couldn't ask him. She had to find another way. She couldn't ask a man who kept three women on his string to escort her to her sister's wedding. Certainly not when they would be expected to sleep in the same room. His other girlfriends would likely object.

As if thinking about them conjured one of them up, a slender brunette stepped out of Will's condo, turning and going up on her toes as Will appeared in the doorway. Great. She got to watch the "good-bye for now, lover" kiss.

The brunette leaned over and kissed Will's cheek. "Give it another twenty minutes and it should be ready. I feel better knowing you have dinner. You don't eat enough."

Poor girl. She was obviously in love, and that was a bad place to be when a dude had two other chicks. She realized she probably looked stupid standing there and started to make her way down the hall. She would ignore all of it and get inside and start looking on Craigslist for a date/potential serial killer. She wondered if the serial killer would let her interview him before her attempted murder.

"Bridget," Will called out.

Damn it. It would be rude not to say anything, but then she was kind of known for being rude. She managed to get to her door, but she hadn't pulled out the key.

"Bridget." He barked her name this time and she couldn't help but respond. The minute he turned that rich, deep baritone on her she was putty.

She forced a smile on her face and turned to see the happy couple. Will had put an arm around the woman who looked to be maybe twenty years old. Will was in his mid-thirties. Pervert. "Hey, I didn't see you there."

"Sure, you didn't. Lisa, this is my neighbor, Bridget," he said.

Lovely Lisa's perfect lips quirked up. "Yeah, I think I know who she is." She stepped away from Will and her perfectly manicured hand came out. "My brother might have mentioned you on more than one occasion."

What? "Your brother?"

"Yep. I am the youngest Daley, and according to my sisters, the most obnoxious, but don't let that fool you. I'm the smart one. Will there is the dunce of the family."

His sisters? She managed to shake the younger woman's hand but her mind was way too busy counting. "Three sisters?"

Lisa nodded as they dropped hands. "Yep. Me, Lila, and Laurel. Our mom wasn't incredibly creative. Well, except when it came to getting her hands on drugs, and then she was brilliant."

"Lisa." It was good to know she wasn't the only one he used that authoritarian, you're-a-dumbass voice on.

He had three sisters and a mom who used drugs? What the hell? She had to know about the sisters. "So you're his sister?"

Lisa's grin widened. "Yes, I might have mentioned that." She turned back to her brother. "She seems surprised. I think she might have been under the mistaken impression that you have a bunch of girlfriends. She

26

doesn't know you very well. He's all about the job, but he's got tonight off and I brought him a ridiculously good lasagna. It's more than enough for everyone. Why don't you stay for dinner?"

Shit. She felt the walls starting to close in. "Oh, I couldn't. I have plans."

Big plans. She was going to open a bottle of wine and feel sorry for herself and then drunk tweet. It was an exciting night for her.

Lisa shook her head and suddenly Bridget found herself being dragged into Will's condo. "Oh, no, you really have to try my lasagna. Will eats like a five-year-old, so I worry he won't appreciate it. And I brought a wine sure to complement it, but the big guy there told me he only drinks beer. Dude, you've been to college and everything. It's time to upgrade the palate."

"You're a meddlesome thing," Will said as he entered the condo. He crossed to the bar and uncorked the wine, pouring it into a glass before handing it to Bridget. "You might as well agree. That one tends to get what she wants."

Bridget took the glass. It looked like she would need the alcohol. "Well, it's okay. It might be nice to have a couple of people to talk to."

Lisa's eyes were lit with mischief as she made her way back to the door. "Oh, it's only Will. I have to leave. I remembered I have a class. Night all. Don't do anything I wouldn't."

Will walked to the door and let his sister out. "I don't even want to know what that means."

She winked his way and he shut the door behind her.

And Bridget felt the trap close. She was alone with Will Daley in his very nicely decorated condo. All alone with him and apparently he didn't have a harem. He had meddlesome sisters and a bad mom. Her curiosity was at war with the deep need to preserve her own dignity. She set the glass down. "Well, I'm sure you have better things to do with your night."

The door locked with a decisive click. "As a matter of fact, I don't. I'm off call and it would be nice to have someone to talk to." He stared at her for a moment. "Do you hate me so much you can't even sit down and have dinner with me, Bridget? What did I do to offend you? I would appreciate the chance to make it up to you."

Yep. The walls were closing in and the ground was shaking under her feet. She decided to go with complete and utter denial. Besides, it was true. She didn't hate him. "I have no idea what you're talking about. I don't have a problem with you. I barely know you."

His eyes narrowed and she worried she'd fallen into another trap. "Yes, that was my point. You barely know me, but you avoid me at every given opportunity, and that seems strange to me when we have so much in common. We live in the same building and have the same friends."

"Lots of people live in the building. I don't spend a ton of time with any of them. Except Mrs. Magnussen. Somehow she corners me at least once a week and tells me about her grandson in Sweden. I think I might have a date with him." She'd seen a picture and unlike most Swedes, Olaf was short and deeply unattractive. She was kind of happy there were whole continents between them.

He crossed to the kitchen and opened the fridge, grabbing a bottle of beer and flipping the top off. "All right. I'll grant you we live in a time when not everyone knows their neighbors, but then we come to the problem of the club. You have to admit you avoid me at Sanctum. We've had what—two whole conversations? I've invited you over here for a drink three times now."

"I was busy." She'd been afraid she would walk into a big old orgy. Except the harem consisted of his sisters.

"You work a lot? I'm going to put together a salad. Romaine or butter lettuce?" He pulled out a big wooden salad bowl.

Unless she wanted to run out of the condo screaming, she wasn't sure how she exited at this point. "Romaine, please. And yes. I have to. My income is directly tied to production, so I'm pretty much always working."

"Writing? You're a writer. You type all day?"

"Among other things. There's more than writing. There's promo and social networking and e-mails and dealing with my agent and publishers." Some days she was lucky to get her word count in.

He worked efficiently, washing his hands and then tearing the lettuce with a precision and grace that spoke of his profession.

"So I heard you're a brain surgeon." She was utterly fascinated with his hands. She couldn't stop watching them. He finished the lettuce and then used a knife to cut the cucumbers.

"I'm a neurosurgeon and Lisa's insane. She's the dumb one. I scored near perfect on my SATs. She was several points behind me."

He was a freaking brain surgeon with a perfect SAT score. She hopped onto his barstool, utterly unwilling to leave now because she sniffed a good story. "Lisa's younger than you."

"Very observant. What gave it away? The frown lines?" He was ridiculously cute when he grinned. With short, dark hair and emerald eyes, he should have been on the cover of a men's fitness magazine, but he also had a brain in that pretty head of his. Yes, that really did do something for her.

"We call those laugh lines where I'm from." She'd talked about using Botox once and Chris and Serena had a fit. They were *her* laugh lines, they'd told her. They were lines she'd earned, soft lines that spoke of a good life. Her mother didn't have a line on her face. She ruthlessly purged them with chemicals and fat from someone else's ass since there wasn't any on hers.

"I like that. Yes, Lisa is ten years younger. Lila is four years younger and Laurel is six. I'm the only boy and significantly older," he explained.

"I have a younger sister." Hey, it was something they had in common.

"How much younger?"

"Amy is five years younger. My parents tried for a boy, but they quit after two girls. Well, I think they tried but I could be wrong. Sometimes I'm certain Amy and I were conceived in some weird science experiment." She'd dreamed of it often. Dreamed that somewhere out there was a loving alien who left her on Earth and she'd been picked up by the wrong traveler. "There are only two of us though. I can't imagine a family of six."

He stopped. "Six?"

"You and your parents and three sisters."

He went back to chopping. He'd moved on to radishes. "No dad in that scenario. I'm pretty sure we all had different fathers."

So the sister hadn't been joking. She could understand bad parents. "Sorry about that."

"Don't be. We all survived."

She really wanted him to talk more. She suddenly had the realization that she'd viewed him as nothing more than a himbo to fantasize about sexually. He was a man. He had problems and baggage, and they might be more like her own than she could imagine. If his sister had been telling the truth, he'd likely had to raise his younger siblings while his mother had chased her demons. Her parents had been far more interested in power and position than they had been in their daughters. "Your sister was saying something about your mom."

There was no way to miss how his muscles tensed. "I don't like to

29

talk about the past. I would much rather discuss the now. You didn't like Lisa until you figured out she was my sister. Did you think she was my lover?"

Heat flashed through her system, and she was sure there was no way she hadn't flushed like crazy. "How was I supposed to know? They don't look like you."

His hair was dark where they had a lightness, more gold and red to their tones and two were quite petite while the third had a willowy grace to her form that didn't scream that she was related to the linebacker in front of Bridget. Will was built on big lines. He had to be six three.

"They? Which one did you think I was sleeping with?" He placed a bowl in front of her. A chuckle huffed from his mouth. "All three? Seriously? You must think I'm far more energetic than I really am. I'm quite lazy. I have a vacation coming up and I'm planning on laying around like a slug."

He had time off? That was convenient.

He refilled her wine glass. Damn. She hadn't noticed she'd emptied it. "No, I'm not dating anyone."

"But you're looking for a sub."

He shrugged again. "Not particularly. I tried that route and it didn't work out for me."

The storyteller in her sensed something juicy. "Then why are you at Sanctum?"

"Why are you at Sanctum?" Will shot back.

Because she wanted to find a man like the ones she wrote about. Because she wanted someone who would love her and see past all the crap she put out there to protect herself. "I'm doing some research."

Yeah. Crap like that. She was so smart.

"There you go. We're both just playing around."

She was heading into her mid-thirties and standing alone with the most gorgeous man she'd ever seen. How long was she going to keep this crap up? The wine had already started to work on her. She knew it was dumb, but she was tired of the self-protective shit, sick of always being the tough girl. "I'm not playing. I'm lying."

"Lying?"

"I don't know. I'm certainly not telling the truth." Why was it so hard to admit it? "I kind of want to see what it would be like to have a Dom."

"Are you serious? Because Mitch told me you've been very academic

30

about it."

"Yeah, that seems safer than opening myself up. Also, the Doms I've worked with haven't called to me. It's not that they're bad. I like Jesse a lot, but he's strictly a friend, and Mitch seems a little cold to me. I would be all over Alex McKay, but the marriage thing is kind of sacred."

"So you don't do married guys?"

She didn't like the hardness in his voice, but she couldn't quite figure out how to respond beyond the obvious. "No. I guess that would be a hard limit. I don't date anyone attached to other people. I don't date a lot at all."

He wiped his hands off on a towel and moved around the bar. "I don't either. Between work and moving, I haven't had a chance and really, I'm not looking for anything serious."

Well, at least he was honest. The one guy she was seriously interested in wasn't serious at all. Story of her life. She nodded. "Understood."

She put the wine glass down.

"Hey, I'm trying to be honest here, so why do I feel like I just became the bad guy?"

She shook her head. "Not at all." It wasn't like he'd offered himself to her. "I think it's good to be upfront and open. You know I really should get to work. I didn't get my word count in today."

She was going to make a fool of herself if she stayed much longer. She liked him. She liked how he talked about his sisters. She liked that he could make a salad and kept making sure she had what she needed. It was a recipe for disaster.

"I thought you were staying for dinner." He moved in, taking up all the space. This close, she could see that he had a five-o'clock shadow across his perfect jaw. She was a sucker for a square jaw. Damn it. Even his ears were hot. She kind of wanted to lick them to see if he was ticklish there.

"I think that's a bad idea."

"Because I'm not looking for anything serious?" Will asked. "Does everything have to be serious? Do you go into every relationship looking to get married?"

"No. I don't think about getting married much." Her parents' marriage was so bad she often couldn't stomach the idea. "But I'm getting too old to do the one-night stand thing."

He moved in closer and she nearly forgot to breathe. He smelled so good. Clean and masculine. Sandalwood. He'd likely washed with it. All over. A vision of him soaping that body made her mouth water. "I didn't say anything about one-night stands. I said maybe you shouldn't take every relationship so seriously. Bridget, I want to spend time with you."

And her nipples were hard. Yeah, they wanted to spend time with him, but her brain was still in charge. "My sister's getting married in Hawaii."

Oh, her brain was a traitor, too.

He loomed over her, his body inches away. His lips curled up in the sexiest grin. "Really? That sounds like fun. When is that happening?"

He was going to kiss her. His lips were going to touch hers and she had the sudden and deep fear that she wouldn't be the same afterward. Still, she couldn't quite seem to move, couldn't get the will worked up to step back. She only managed to run her tongue across her lips to make sure they weren't bone dry. "Soon. Next week."

He sighed, his hands finding her shoulders. "Oh, I guess you're going to be out of town then. I was hoping to see you while I was on vacation next week."

She was mesmerized by his eyes. This close, she could see how green they were. His hands moved to her neck. "You could come with me. I need a date."

Now she was kind of happy everyone else had turned her down. It seemed right to ask him, good to be here with him.

There was the sound of a phone ringing.

He shook his head as his hands sank into her hair. The way he was taking his time did something for her. The men she'd been with before had all just gone for it and would likely have already been pawing her boobs by now, but Will was moving with languid seduction. It was like a dance. "You need a date?"

The only thing pulling her out of the sensual haze was that stupid phone. Who had a landline these days? "I do. Shouldn't you get that?"

His nose touched hers as his fingers ran along her scalp, sending pleasurable shivers through her body. "Don't worry about it. The hospital requires I keep a house phone. And a pager. And a cell. If it's really important, they'll page me. This is more fun than answering the phone, don't you think? Bridget, you know I won't be able to keep my hands off you if we go to Hawaii together."

She didn't want him to. She was fairly certain she was going to fall into bed with him in the next ten minutes. Maybe he was right. Maybe she took everything too seriously and she should have some fun for once in her life. Maybe she could handle it. "Will?"

His mouth hovered right over hers, and there was no way to mistake the satisfaction coming off him. He wanted her. God, he really wanted her. "Yes, Bridget?"

"Do you want to come to Hawaii with me? We could have fun." She would understand that it was temporary. Or maybe it was a way to get to know each other. Maybe to find out if they were compatible.

"Hey, Will. It's Mitch. I couldn't get you on your cell. I wanted to let you know that I talked to Jace and he has agreed to be conveniently unable to travel for the next couple of weeks. That's the last of them and it should be smooth sailing for you. If Bratty Bridget wants a date, she's going to have to come to you. According to the report my investigator did on her, there's no one else she can go to unless she wants to call her loser ex-boyfriend."

He reached over and picked up the phone and slammed the receiver back down.

Bridget froze, the words pouring over her like icy rain.

She'd spent days going hat in hand to the Doms of Sanctum and she'd never stood a chance. Not with any of them.

"All right. I'm hoping you view this as something kind of flattering. I mean, I did go to a lot of trouble to make sure I was the last guy standing." He tried to move back in.

Bridget stepped away, putting her hands up. "Somehow I don't see it as flattering. And Bratty Bridget? Is that what everyone calls me behind my back?"

"You can't argue with it. Everyone's come up against that mouth of yours."

"Is that what this is about? You want to show everyone that you can take me down a peg?" She was not going to cry. She didn't fucking cry. She'd learned it didn't buy her anything, not even peace since her father would "give her something to cry about" when she did. "Fuck you, Daley."

She turned and started for the door.

* * * *

He was going to kill Mitch. The bastard had the worst timing ever and he was so fucking impatient. If the son of a bitch had left a message on his cell like the rest of the world, he would be kissing Bridget right now. He'd been so close. He would have gone slow, made her feel comfortable. All the while he would have been maneuvering her straight to bed. He would have wined and dined her and woken up beside her the next day.

Now he had to make sure she didn't murder him in his sleep.

"Hey, we're not done." He tried his most authoritative voice on her.

She reached the door. "Oh, we're done. You can bite my ass, Doc."

She slammed the door open and began storming out, proving she really did know how to make an exit. Dramatic. That was one way to describe it.

He reached her in three strides, taking her elbow in his hand and turning her around. "I'm sorry you heard that."

Her face was flushed to an embarrassed pink, but she'd shoved a wall up the minute she'd heard that message and now he couldn't read her emotions. When he'd been close, he'd watched as desire and something like longing had played across her pretty face. She'd started to open to him and now the castle defenses were firmly back in place.

"I'm sorry I ever met you." Yes. Bratty Bridget was back.

"Come on. What was I supposed to do? You wouldn't give me the time of day." He had very few places to go since he really was the dick in this scenario. He'd done the crime and gotten caught. He had to find a way to plead his case because now that he'd been so close to her, he knew he couldn't let it go. If she hadn't responded to him, hadn't opened up, he would have admired her from afar. But that wasn't what happened.

"You know what you're supposed to do? You're supposed to take the fucking hint, Daley. Not interested."

It made him crazy. She was lying. He'd seen the way she softened. "You're pissed off and I understand that, but not a one of those men would take care of you the way I will."

Her eyes rolled. "Of course. None of them could possibly be interested in me. Guess what? I wasn't looking for passion out of this. I was trying to find a man to be my date. I wasn't trying to find a lover."

She was so naïve. "You can't invite a man to stay in a hotel with you and expect him to keep his hands to himself."

"Why not? Are you all animals? Do you run around raping any woman you want?"

"Of course not, but every fucking Dom at Sanctum would attempt to seduce you and I don't want that. I want to be the one who seduces you. I want to be the one who sees if you can purr." That was about as honest as he could get. "Bridget, tell me you feel this chemistry for another guy and I'll go talk to him myself. I'll make sure he can go with you."

A calculated risk. She'd already proven she could lie when she wanted to. If she did, he would have to go with it.

But her body was already coming close to his as though they were magnetized. She could spout bile all she liked, but her body responded to his. "I'm not looking for chemistry. I simply want a nice guy to help me out."

"I'll help you. You want someone to play your fiancé and all parents love me. I'll be your successful, supportive fake future husband. I'll let you dress me and I'll charm those nasty cousins of yours until they all want what you have."

The cutest look flashed across her face. She was even lovely when she was annoyed with him. "You know about my cousins?"

The whole while he was backing her up, leading her to the wall so she wouldn't have anywhere else to go. "I eavesdropped. That should tell you how pathetic I am about you."

"Or what a freaky stalker you are." Her back was against the wall and there was no way to miss the hitch in her breath.

"You are pessimistic, sweetheart. Why can't you see it as quirky and charming? I swear I've never stalked anyone before. You're my first." Maybe she would see that as adorable.

She shook her head. "Try it on another girl. I'm not buying it."

So frustrating. "Let me kiss you. One kiss and if you don't want me as much as I want you, I'll walk away. But you won't find anyone as perfect as me for this job of yours. I can give you my full attention, baby. I can make it my goal in life to ensure that everyone thinks you're the luckiest girl on earth by the end of that wedding, and you know what else?"

Her hands had gone to his waist. She'd already made the decision. He knew he would get his one shot with her. Excitement built in his gut and his dick was already hard as a rock.

"What else, Daley?"

"I'll be your Dom. I'll show you what it means. Any questions you have, I'll answer. We'll sign a short-term contract and by the end, you'll know for sure if you want to find a permanent Dom. Hell, I'll help you find one if that's what you want."

Something passed over her face, almost a sadness, but he couldn't be sure because she was so good at hiding it. Her chin came up stubbornly. "All right then. Kiss me."

Suddenly he wished he'd talked her back into his condo, wished he'd been able to sit and eat with her. He wanted more time and he wasn't even sure why. Up to this point, all he'd required was her body, but now he realized she was more than a glorious set of tits and a heart-shaped ass.

She was a mystery.

He leaned over because he wasn't going to get more time. He had roughly two minutes to tempt her into something that likely wouldn't be good for her. He was a bastard and he knew it and he still couldn't stop his head from dropping. His lips pressed against hers and warmth poured through him. He let his hands find her waist. He wasn't going to go straight for her ass. He hadn't earned it.

Gently he molded his lips against hers, savoring the sensation. He could fucking eat her up. She was wearing some kind of lip balm, something sweet. Whatever it was, he couldn't get enough of it. He ate at her mouth, softly running his lips over hers and giving her the barest hint of his tongue. He didn't want to scare her with what his every instinct told him to do. He wouldn't have dreamed of it, but there was a caveman deep inside him, and cavedick wanted to drag her back to his bed and make sure she couldn't leave it come morning.

He wasn't that guy. He was civilized, educated. He didn't get addicted to anything. Anything. He wasn't about to get addicted to a sweet brat who would make him crazy. Peace. He needed peace and he wouldn't get it from her.

Not that he wanted peace in that moment. He wanted inside her. Every cell in his body was singing like it never had before. She stirred him.

Bridget sighed and softened against him and he stopped thinking. Only one thing mattered and that was the feel of her in his arms, the way she moaned into his mouth. Her jaw dropped slightly and he was inside, his tongue playing against hers. So soft. Everything about her was so damn soft.

He dragged her hard against his body, no longer worried about frightening her. She needed to know what he could offer. He could give her the dominance she craved. His cock pressed to her belly and rubbed against her like a cat seeking affection. Her hands clutched at him as she gave as good as she got.

Pure fire threatened to take over. He didn't need a bed. He could fuck her right here in the hallway. He could drop his jeans and he wouldn't care who watched.

Before he reached for her breasts, she put a hand between them.

"Stop." Her voice was husky, out of breath.

Fuck. He took a step back because he wasn't sure he would be capable of following her very clear order. His damn hands were shaking. "All right."

She took a long breath and seemed to compose herself. "I'll admit, physically it seems like we're compatible."

"We're explosive, Bridget." He'd never had that reaction to another woman. He wasn't sure he liked it, but he couldn't seem to stop.

"That doesn't mean this is good for either of us. I don't like being manipulated, Daley."

"Call me Will." He wasn't dumb. He'd taken enough psych classes to know when a person was distancing. He couldn't allow it.

She slipped by him and started going through her purse. In seconds she had the key out. "Fine. I don't like being manipulated, Will."

A pit opened up in his gut. He forced himself to walk back to his own door. "Answer me this. Would you have asked me? Would you have ever let me kiss you?"

"No."

"Then at least I got my shot." He was used to having to fight for the things he wanted. He'd been doing it since he was born.

She opened the door, but her eyes stayed on him. "I need to think about it. Can I have a couple of days?"

She wasn't outright rejecting him? "Sure. My schedule's open. I won't change that. I really can help you, Bridget."

"I'm not so sure about that. I'll get back to you." She disappeared behind her door.

He wasn't out yet. He still had a shot, but it was going to be a long couple of days.

His phone rang again. His cell this time. Damn it. He wasn't on call. He should get a little bit of peace. He shut and locked the door and crossed the floor to grab his cell. He didn't recognize the number, but answered anyway. Sometimes Laurel forgot to charge her phone. His sisters were the real reason he always answered his damn phone. He'd spent his whole life watching out for them and now he couldn't quite stop.

"Hello?"

"Will?"

He went still because he recognized that voice. He didn't want to believe it was true. "This is Doctor Daley. Who is this?"

A sniffle came over the line. "Will, it's Starr."

He hung up immediately.

He was going to have to change his number. He quickly dialed Mitch's phone and was happy when he picked up on the first ring. Will didn't wait for his voice to come over the line. "Why the fuck is she out of jail?"

"Well, hello to you, Doctor Daley. You're in a good mood."

"I got a call from Leslie Starling." Starr's real name. She'd told him she preferred Starr because they twinkled so brightly and she wanted to be something pretty.

He'd met her at the first club he'd gone to. He hadn't been able to resist his needs a second longer. That club had been a hellhole compared to Sanctum, but he'd felt at home the minute he took a class and picked up a flogger. He'd finally found a place he belonged and then she'd shown up. Lovely and deeply submissive, she'd brought him a certain peace. She'd needed him.

She'd been lying all the while.

He could still feel the needle in his neck, the pain flaring before something so much sweeter took its place. Heroin. They'd given him heroin.

He still thought about it.

"Shit. The prison allowed her to call you? Are you fucking kidding me?" Mitch's voice grounded him. "All right. First, I'm going to call and have the warden's ass and then I'm going to make sure every guard at that prison knows her status. I can get a restraining order even while she's waiting trial."

He forced himself to calm. He wasn't truly afraid of a five foot nothing girl. He was afraid of what she'd done to him. She'd taken his control. She'd shown him how good it could be to float away. Like his mother had. He'd always known he was a time bomb waiting to go off. "She wasn't calling from prison. Trust me. I know there's a protocol to be followed when one calls from prison."

His mother had called every time she got arrested. She would call and

38

beg him to make her bail. He'd started getting those calls when he was ten years old and every time a voice came over the phone requesting that he take a call from so and so prison or jail. He still got those damn calls at least once a month. Starr's voice hadn't been preceded by anything. Starr was out. She was walking the streets.

"All right. First, I'll find out what's happening on my way to your place," Mitch said.

"You don't have to come here."

"Yes, I do because this is going to get to you. You're going to think about it and you need someone around to talk to. We'll sit and watch the game and order a pizza. Unless you have other plans."

Something eased in his gut. He really would rather have company. "No pizza. Lisa made dinner and no, I don't have plans, you bastard. I almost had Bridget but guess who called right before I got to the good stuff?"

"Shit. You need to get rid of that answering machine. Join the twenty-first century."

"I'm not completely out yet. She's thinking about it, but you owe me."

"Anything for my favorite client." Mitch had been the one to smooth the way with the police after the "incident." Even though the cop involved knew Will was innocent, there was still paperwork to be done and questions to be answered. Mitch had shown up, offered his services, and they'd become friends. Mitch was the one who convinced him to give Sanctum a chance.

"Get your ass over here so I can punch you in the face."

"On my way." The phone hung up and Will was alone again.

But not entirely. He'd learned to take stock of what was good. He breathed in the smell of the lasagna. His sister had made it for him. She'd turned into an amazing young woman. He looked over at Bridget's wine glass and the salad he'd made. She hadn't said no. And Mitch was on his way.

He was in control. He wasn't going to end up some crazed addict, because he had things to live for and getting inside Bridget was definitely one of them.

He pulled the lasagna out and quickly made her a plate. He placed it on a tray along with a couple of cookies he'd bought at the bakery down the street. He wrote a quick note about wanting to make sure she ate a decent meal. He took it out the door and set it in front of hers. After pressing the doorbell, he stepped back into his condo and shut the door.

He couldn't help watching her through his peephole and he didn't miss the way she smiled.

He really had to stop the creepy-stalker stuff, but he was smiling, too.

Chapter Three

"Are you serious? He blackmailed every Dom in the club so that he could have you all to himself?" Serena asked before she downed a mini quiche. "That's so romantic."

Bridget looked around the small party at Grace Taggart's house to see if someone was listening in. The subs were all here, all in their prettiest dresses and heels, and she felt like a troll.

"It is kind of sweet if you think about it." Chris had driven her here. It was the weekly girls' night—though that was kind of sexist. She amended the statement in her head. Weekly sub night. There were two whole guys at the party. Chris and Mistress Jackie's sub, Harold, though he seemed to gasp at every single statement made.

"He's kind of totally into you," Serena said.

"He's kind of an asshole," Bridget tossed back. She also tossed back a shot of tequila. She definitely needed the alcohol. "But his sister is a great cook."

"So you did have dinner with him." Chris leaned forward. "Do you know if he can cook? If he can cook in the kitchen, he can probably cook in the bedroom."

Had it only been last night that she'd found out what an asswipe Will Daley was? And then what a creepy-stalker kind of sweet guy he was who made sure she ate something? "No. He made me a tray and left it outside of my door."

"So it could have been an evil tray and yet you ate it," Chris pointed out. "He's got you seriously turned around because you're usually paranoid about everything."

She would have protested but he knew her well. "I ate the whole thing. I knew it was him. Am I being an idiot?"

"No," Serena said.

"Yes," Chris replied.

It was good that they were in harmony. "I know I shouldn't even consider it, but I am. I can't help it. He's kind of put me in a corner."

Or against a wall. She'd thought all night about how he'd shoved her against that wall and crowded her before he'd lowered his lips down and taken her mouth like she'd only dreamed of before. She hadn't been able to think when he had his hands on her. She'd been lucky he'd taken her seriously when she'd told him to stop because if he'd pressed his case, she might have gone under.

She might have ended up with her legs spread wide, pleading for him to put that big cock inside her. God, it had felt big. It had pressed against her belly and tempted her to find out what sex really felt like.

She was pretty sure it wasn't a yawn. Not with Will Daley.

"Because no one else will go?" Chris asked. "I can find someone for you. I can walk right into the Tin Room and find you a date."

The Tin Room was Dallas's infamous gay strip club. Bridget was fairly certain Chris could definitely find her a date there for a price. The man would be gorgeous and have a perfect body and want nothing but cash from her.

Will was offering to give her something in return. He was offering to introduce her to D/s. She could figure out if she really wanted what she wrote about. She'd talked to lots of couples, played around a little, but D/s had always been a metaphor in her books. It was a way to talk about communication between lovers.

"I'll think about it," she muttered as Karina walked in the room. The gorgeous dark-haired woman had brought a friend with her, though they seemed a bit awkward together. Karina was lushly curved and her blonde friend looked like a starving Nordic supermodel. "I'm going to go talk to Karina. I'll be right back."

"She's going to ask her about Will," Chris said.

"Yes, she is," Serena replied.

"No, I'm not." She sighed. "Fine. I am since no one else will talk about it."

She strode over to where Karina was ordering a club soda and her friend was ogling the bartender. "Hey, Karina, can I talk to you for a minute?"

Karina gave her a sure smile. "Of course."

"I need a diet soda and skinny vodka, heavy on the vodka. Actually just give me the vodka. We'll call it a martini," the blonde said.

"Olives?" the bartender asked.

The blonde winked his way. "Only if I'm eating them off your body, honey. I don't eat anything without some sort of physical activity. When do you get off? Work I mean. Because I can get you off three minutes after that. Seriously. My oral technique is superlative."

Bridget watched them with a sort of shocked fascination.

"Maia, you promised," Karina whispered.

Maia shrugged. "I promised I would try. I left the driver intact and he was lovely." A long sigh came from her perfectly painted mouth. "Fine. But I thought this would be more fun."

The bartender held up his hands, a wide-eyed look on his face. "I'm gay."

"I could fix that for you," Maia replied and then turned away. "Fine. But I don't see how my not getting any is supposed to do anything but put me in a bad mood. You, entertain me."

Bridget realized the rude blonde was talking to her. "You, go fuck yourself."

A wide smile crossed the blonde's lips. "Oh, I like this one, Karina."

"Ignore her. She did Big Tag a massive favor and now we all have to put up with her for a year. I kind of want to kill Tag for that. I'm babysitting."

"I did a favor for you, too," Maia said irritably as she picked up her martini. "I handed you Derek on a silver platter. And I don't need a babysitter."

"Fine, I'm monitoring the beast," Karina conceded.

"I like that so much better." Maia looked out over the gathering.

Bridget really didn't want to know more. "I wanted to talk to you about Will."

Maia's eyes lit up. "The good doctor? The ridiculously naïve one who almost got everyone killed a couple of months back? He had a very nice ass."

She didn't like the idea of Skeletor looking at Will's ass, but she couldn't miss the salient point. "Almost got everyone killed?"

Karina frowned. "That's overstating it a little."

"Well, they weren't going to kill him. They were leaving him alive to take the fall for killing you. That man is superhot but he's dumb as a post," Maia said. "Actually that's kind of how I like them. So beautiful. So very stupid. I should look him up."

Bridget had enough of Maia. "He isn't stupid. He's a freaking neurosurgeon. What the hell are you? Some kind of dumbass, can't do anything but smile for the camera model?"

Maia put a hand on her arm. "That's so sweet. I always thought I could model. No. I'm assistant district attorney for Dallas County and I'm the one who got your crush out of the mess he'd gotten himself into. He had his perfect sub but she turned out to be using him. What he saw in that no-brain idiot, I have no idea."

Karina put a hand up. "Maia, there's Eve. Why don't you go and bug her?"

Maia nodded. "Oh, those shoes. Yes, someone should tell her they make her look like a milkmaid. And that hair. Horrible. She needs an intervention."

"Is that a good idea?" Bridget liked Eve. It seemed a horrible thing to sick a blonde demon on her.

"Eve finds her amusing. I believe she's writing an academic paper on Maia as the new Narcissus." Karina turned sympathetic eyes on her. "You're interested in Will?"

Interested? Was she interested in a man she couldn't stop thinking about? She'd tried to write this morning and her blond cowboy hero kept turning into a dark-haired doctor. "I'm considering going out with him."

For a limited time.

"He's a good guy. I met him while I was working a case having to do with missing girls."

"Was he a suspect? Because I can't see him physically hurting anyone." He might break her heart, but she'd been safe with him. The minute she'd shown a hint of pulling back, he'd respected her decision.

"Only in Derek's mind," she said with a wink. "Derek was jealous, but I always knew Will was a well-meaning man. We met him in a club. Not a good one, but then he was testing the waters. I think he tried to hide his dominant needs for a very long time. He even had a cover story. He pretended to be an EMT so no one from the hospital he worked at would find out. I get the feeling there's a lot Will likes to hide from the world."

"Do you know about his mom?"

"Only after the fact. I dug into his background. He grew up really poor, Bridget. He's likely not proud of the fact that he came from a trailer park and his mom was in and out of jail."

He needed to be in control because so much of his life had been out of it. "He should be proud. He's come a long way."

"I happen to know for a fact that it never feels far away," Karina said, her eyes softening. "When you come from someplace like that it always feels like you're one step away from being right back there. Will isn't hiding anymore. He changed hospitals and while he's private, he's not actively hiding now. I know he's talked to his sisters about going to clubs."

"And they didn't have a problem with it?" Lisa didn't seem to have a single problem with her brother.

"They adore him. He could murder someone and they would ask how they could help him. He raised them. He protected them. He had two jobs from the time he was fourteen and he got through school. He's a hell of a guy, but I worry he still doesn't know what he wants."

He knew what he wanted when it came to her. He wanted a couple of weeks of casual fun. Was there really anything wrong with that? She hadn't had sex in a year. Since she'd kicked her no-good boyfriend to the curb, she'd lived like a nun. "The evil one said something about him having a sub?"

"Her name was Starr," Karina replied. "Well, she called herself that. She was more like a slave than a sub."

"That's what he wants?" She couldn't do that, couldn't suppress her own needs to give everything to some man no matter how good his abs looked. She'd met some of those women and a few she genuinely believed were happy, but it wasn't for her.

"Like I said, he was exploring. Most Doms go through a phase where they want a very submissive playmate. And a whole bunch of them come to the conclusion that they would rather have a full partner. It works for some people. You know the saying. There are as many ways to practice D/s as there are people who practice it. Some people look at it like a religion and some of us adapt it to fit our needs. It's simply a more open way for two partners to use their strengths and buoy each other's weaknesses. Will came from a place where everyone was dependent on him. He's comfortable handling the whole load, but that's not necessarily what he needs."

"I don't know what I need either," Bridget admitted. "I thought I needed stability and that led me to stay with a man who cheated on me for years. Maybe I need to follow my instincts this time." And not give in to her fear that she was going to be the fool again.

"I think you could be good for Will, but I would advise you to take it slow."

Slow. She didn't have time to take it slow. Her cell chirped. Her sister. Damn it. "Thanks, Karina. I'll think about what you said. I have to take this."

Karina nodded. "I'll go save Eve. Oh look. Charlotte Taggart threw a glass of water at Maia. Don't you fight! She's pregnant!"

Karina hurried off to stop the chick fight.

Bridget flipped her phone to answer it. "Hey, Amy."

"Hey, big sis. I wanted to let you know that I got the private jet set up for you. I e-mailed all the details."

"I know. I want to thank you for that. I kind of thought Pops would force me to fly commercial." It would be considered a huge indignity in her father's eyes.

"I handled it. Besides, everyone's interested in seeing who you bring. By the way, did I apologize profusely for doing that to you? I was slightly tipsy. It was either that or I would have thrown a punch and I'd recently gotten my nails done."

Was she actually going to do this? What was she thinking? She should hire her gay stripper and be happy with him. "I found someone."

"All right. Now all we have to do is come up with a cover story. I'm thinking Harvard educated something. Dad always loves Harvard educated people."

"Nope. He doesn't need a cover. He's a doctor."

And just like that she knew there was no going back. Two weeks. She had two weeks to pretend, to explore, to discover.

46

Maybe two weeks were better than nothing.

* * * *

The next afternoon Will moved across the basketball court, his hands out and ready for the pass. Sweat dripped from his brow, but he welcomed it. He needed to sweat for some reason other than his dick being in a constant state of erection. Maybe if he worked his body hard enough he wouldn't think about Bridget's breasts crushed to his chest or the way her lips felt against his.

He'd slept like crap for two nights, waiting for her to call. She still hadn't said no, but he was starting to think silence was his answer.

He took his shot, and unlike the one he'd taken with Bridget, this time his aim was true. The ball swooshed into the net.

"Alex! How about some defense?" Ian Taggart shouted across the court.

Alex McKay shot his friend the finger after grabbing the ball. "Give an old man a break. We're down by five and I have to meet Eve in thirty minutes. I need a shower."

"Pussy. Eve should appreciate your manly sweat," Taggart said, running a hand through his hair. "Kai, find me a tall dude who doesn't mind tossing his body around. Alex won't even throw an elbow anymore."

Kai snorted as he shook his head. "I think Alex would mention that this is supposed to be a friendly game and he's showing his emotional maturity by treating it that way."

"Yeah, well, it sucks to lose." Taggart turned his icy gaze Will's way. "Who let you in anyway?"

"I think that was you." He'd learned that the only way to handle Taggart was to speak his language. Which seemed to be sarcasm. "You should improve your vetting process. Don't feel bad. I got through my undergraduate work on a basketball scholarship."

Two jobs. Basketball practice. Making sure his sisters were fed and did their homework. Yeah, he didn't miss those days, but they hadn't left a ton of time for him to worry. He'd had to keep moving.

Bridget had likely had tutors and housekeepers and a massive college fund.

Two different worlds. Maybe it was for the best.

"You, Kai, do your job and find me some short, unathletic assholes

Alex can defend against. I can't drop him because he's old and soft." Taggart's loyalty was something to be admired.

Alex McKay grinned as he backed toward the door that led into Sanctum. "I'm just glad Charlotte put an end to Ian's dream of putting a boxing ring in. He's trying to take his anxieties out on my body."

Kai turned to Taggart. "You should really spend some time on my couch, Ian. We could talk out your fears about becoming a father."

Ian ignored Kai. "I don't need a ring. We could start a fight club without a damn ring. What's the first rule of fight club?"

Will knew that one. "No one talks about fight club."

"No, the first person to mention my anxieties gets his nose broken. This is my fucking fight club. I make the rules." Big Tag stalked inside the club.

Kai rolled his eyes. "Sometimes I wonder why I'm here. In exchange for him footing the bill for my pro bono work, he gave me a list of applicants and then unapproved the only one who was suitable. Do you know what his reasoning was?"

With Taggart, no one could be sure. But Will decided to cut the guy some slack since he was funding Kai's practice. Kai specialized in the treatment of PTSD in soldiers returning from war. Taggart had renovated the previously unused second floor of Sanctum, and now a steady stream of former servicemen made their way to weekly sessions with Kai. "No idea, man. I wouldn't even try to come up with one."

Kai sat down on the bench that overlooked the small court. Someone had taken the space and turned it into a small garden, a tiny oasis of green. The place was fenced in, but buildings rose from all around, reminding Will he was in the city. Will stretched while Kai let his head fall back, obviously enjoying the sun. "He told me he would never have a Dom named Devinshea in his club because it was a douchebag name."

Will snorted a little. "He's got a point."

A laugh came from Kai's mouth. "He said that if this dude's parents had wanted him to have a membership at Sanctum, they should have named him something more masculine like Frank or Dan." Kai shook his head with a sigh. "That man has serious issues."

"Yes, his name is Devinshea." He was kind of with Taggart on that one. Poor dude probably got his ass kicked on a regular basis. He didn't mention that Kai wasn't a hell of a lot better. Sometimes he was happy his mother wasn't terribly creative. She'd named him after his dad and then went down a list of *L* names with his sisters.

"No. I'm talking about Taggart. I think he's scared of becoming a dad. It can't be easy for him. His own father left at a young age." Kai's eyes were suddenly on him. "It can't be easy taking on an adult role when you're still a kid. That kind of responsibility can be difficult to deal with. It can cause a person to go through a kind of arrested development."

Jeez. And they were back to him. "We're not talking about Taggart anymore."

Kai didn't deny it. "I heard about the scam you ran on Bridget Slaten. I was surprised you would do that. I've been trying to figure out why you want to hurt her like that. You've never come off as a cruel person."

"I'm not trying to hurt her. I was trying to herd her to me."

Kai's brow rose in a surprised arch. "Really?"

"I was trying to get laid, dude."

"Huh. Well, then that's a different story, though I'm pretty sure it still has the same ending."

He was a bit offended Kai thought he was actively trying to be an asshole. "You thought I was trying to hurt her?"

"Well, I certainly didn't think you were trying to date her. You have to admit that when you discuss your perfect woman, it wouldn't be her."

For some reason that didn't set well with him. "She's not so bad."

"I didn't say she was bad. I quite like her. She's refreshingly honest about most things, but she's also quite independent. I think you might chafe against that independence. You told me you would prefer a woman who was somewhat dependent on you."

"I don't think I put it like that. I think I talked about enjoying a submissive lover. I like to be in control. It's kind of the whole point of being a Dom. If I didn't need control, I would be vanilla or into swinging or foot fetishes or something." Though he often thought it would be simpler if he only wanted to suck on a chick's toes.

"I got the feeling you would prefer a woman who was submissive out of the bedroom as well. Bridget is never going to be that woman. In her own way, she needs control as much as you do. I believe she requires submission in order to let go long enough to find pleasure sexually. In some ways she almost needs permission to find pleasure or relaxation of any kind."

It didn't make sense to him. She'd grown up ridiculously wealthy. Her childhood would have been marked by opportunity.

Was it possible that she might need him?

"Are you sure this is a good idea?" Kai asked. "I worry Bridget needs more than you're willing to give any woman at this point."

Sometimes Kai could be annoying. Will wondered if it would be rude to walk away. Probably. And he did kind of consider the guy a friend. "How do you know what I'm willing to give a woman?"

"Because we have weekly sessions and I did the whole PhD thing. Should I go over my credentials?"

"When do those end, by the way?" In order to get into Sanctum, he had to agree to weekly sessions with the good doc for a prescribed period of time.

"You're on probation for six months. I'll clear you at the end unless something changes radically, but I hope you consider continuing the sessions. I think it's good for you to have a place where you can talk."

He would never admit it, but he enjoyed those stupid sessions. Kai was right. It was good to talk. He'd told Kai things he'd never talked about before. Something about the man…well, he trusted Kai. "We'll see, but I don't understand how I'm hurting Bridget."

Kai's dark eyes brightened and he leaned in. "I'm so glad you asked."

"I wish I hadn't." He knew a trap when he fell into one.

"But you did. Look, I think Bridget needs someone who can be serious about her."

He was totally serious about fucking her. "From what I can tell she's not dating. If she's not in a relationship, I don't see what's wrong with spending some time with me. I've explained everything to her. I've been honest about what I want. If she decides to go to bed with me, it's because she wants to."

Kai pointed at him as though he'd made a point. "That's the thing. I don't know that she's truly capable of stating what she wants. There's a lot in her background that taught her to isolate herself and her needs. She won't let you see when she's upset."

Was he high? "Have you seen what happens to people who cut her off on the highway? I was behind her once and she is the very definition of road rage. I heard a story from Serena about the way she deals with assholes who try to get out of traffic by driving in the service lane. She throws the passenger door open, man. I can't imagine what her insurance premiums are like. I don't think she has a problem expressing herself."

"Anger, no. She can express that readily. Hurt? Vulnerability? Those

50

are different. You're a good guy, Will. You recently came off a bad relationship."

"If by bad you mean she tried to set me up for murder, then yes, it was bad." It still sat in his gut. How stupid he'd been. Naïve and foolish. He didn't want Bridget to ever find out how dumb he'd been.

"You've still got a lot of anger and I don't want you taking it out on Bridget," Kai explained. "She seems like an easy target because she's so prickly, but underneath she's quite soft. You know she's the black sheep of her family, right?"

She never talked about her family from what he could tell. "Why?"

"I think it has something to do with her chosen profession."

The sex books. Her father was probably a stick in the mud and didn't like that his daughter wrote sex for a living. "Her father is a public figure. I'm sure having a daughter who writes porn is a liability."

Kai's eyes widened. "Do not call it that if you want to hold on to your balls."

"Porn?" What else was he supposed to call it? Girl porn?

"Yeah, they take offense," Kai said. "Read her books. If you want to know who she is, read one of her books. I don't think you'll call it porn then. And you might have some more sympathy for her."

He hated feeling restless and that was what this whole conversation was doing to him. The last thing he wanted to do was cause Bridget harm. "You really think having a short-term affair will hurt her?"

Kai nodded. "I think she needs more."

"All right." He wasn't a bad guy, but he had to be better. "I'll find her a date. Any way you could go to Hawaii next week?"

"I would love to. I genuinely like Bridget, but I'm not ready for a relationship either so I'll keep my hands off her. I think you're doing the right thing, Will. Give it some time and you'll find the other side. You'll come out of this and you'll be ready for something real."

The door opened and Will turned, ready to see Taggart or McKay.

"Will?" Bridget put a hand over her eyes, obviously adjusting to the bright light of the afternoon.

She was here. She was standing there in a white shirt and jeans and those strappy sandals she liked to wear. Her dark hair was loose and flowing.

He was a good man. He always did the right thing. He stood up. "Hey, I'm glad you're here."

He trusted Kai. Kai knew what he was talking about. When Starr had called two nights before, there had been rage in his gut at the very thought of her. He wasn't in a place to give Bridget a fair shake. She needed someone who she might have a shot with. The very fact that it had run through his head that a woman didn't give a damn about anything but sex was proof positive he wasn't thinking straight.

She brushed her hair back and seemed to steel herself. "I tried calling you. For a guy with two phones, you don't answer a lot."

"It's in the locker. I was playing basketball. Keeping your phone in your pocket is a very good way to destroy it. Despite what Taggart will tell you, McKay hits pretty hard." He was putting off the inevitable. He didn't want to break it off. When he told her he was letting her go, she would retreat. She wouldn't brush it off and tell them they could be friends.

He didn't want to be her friend. Damn it. He hated being a good fucking person in that moment.

Of course, it likely wouldn't matter because from the grim look on her face, she'd come to give him her answer.

"Well, I probably should tell you this in person."

Getting rejected sucked even when he'd been about to reject her in the first place. He hadn't realized how much he'd counted on her saying yes to him. Since the moment he'd seen her, he'd plotted and planned on having her, and now that restless feeling threatened to take over. He would have to throw himself into work, but he'd taken all that time off. Still, letting her off the hook was the right thing to do. "You don't have to say it."

He would let Kai take care of her, and she would have a good time. She wouldn't get any orgasms out of Kai, and Kai would likely only talk to her about the lifestyle in an academic fashion. He wouldn't tie her up so she would know what it felt like to take her Dom's cock up her ass.

Damn it. He was fucking hard again, and masturbating was a poor substitute for the real thing.

She closed her eyes, and her shoulders came up around her ears. "Yes."

Well, he'd known it. "I was talking to Kai and we thought…" What? "Yes?"

Kai stood. "Bridget, Will and I have been talking."

"About how great it's going to be to go to Hawaii," he said quickly. She said yes. Yes. She'd said yes to him even knowing what the boundaries of the relationship were.

"What happened to being a good person?" Kai asked under his breath.

Good people apparently didn't get inside Bridget. His cock had heard the word yes and his conscience had become an unnecessary thing. She'd said yes.

He was going to be her Dom.

He moved into her space, a lightness he hadn't felt in forever taking over. Thinking of nothing but getting close to her, he wrapped his arms around her and lifted her up, hauling her close as he pressed his lips to hers. "You said yes."

Her arms found their way around his neck, and she smiled the first pure smile he'd seen from her. It was joyous, without the edge of cynicism that seemed to accompany everything she did. He'd put that smile on her face.

"I said yes, but I thought you would be cleaner," she said, wrinkling her nose. She didn't push him away though. She seemed perfectly content to dangle in his arms.

"Don't worry about that, baby. According to Taggart, it's just a little manly sweat and I promise to shower before tonight." He kissed her again, lightly with no real intent but showing her affection.

He had time with her.

"Tonight?"

"Dinner. My place. We have a contract to write." The minute her signature was on that sucker, he would be all over her. Not that he wasn't already. He finally put her down, but kept his hands on her waist, unwilling to give up contact.

Her eyes lit up. "I have a hundred questions about contracts. Do you have a standard? Or do you write a new one each time? Will we be going over hard and soft limits? When I joined Sanctum, I had to sign a contract. Will it be like that one?"

Being in a relationship with a writer was going to be different. Bridget was full of an infectious curiosity. Her enthusiasm flowed into him, and something that seemed boring and formal might be fun. Starr hadn't asked a single question about their contract. She'd signed and then spread her legs and he'd thought that meant she loved him.

He stopped himself because he wasn't going there. Kai was wrong. He wasn't trying to take out his anger on Bridget. It was pure lust and she'd said yes. Besides, he had something to give her. He had knowledge.

"I'll answer every question you have. I'm your Dom for the next couple of weeks and I promise I'll be an open book when it comes to the lifestyle. We'll play and you'll get lots of material for your books."

She blushed, a pretty pink staining her cheeks. "Okay. I'll see you tonight."

He watched her walk away, a hunger deep in his gut. He couldn't remember being so fucking hungry.

"So, you decided to go a different way." Kai was looking up at him with judgmental eyes. "I take it that was an argument between your conscience and your penis, and your penis seems to have won."

"What can I say, Doc? My penis made a logical argument." He stared at the door and couldn't stop thinking about the evening to come.

Chapter Four

It was surreal, but she was staring at a contract that had been written for her. A real live D/s contract with her name on it. It was different from the training contract she'd signed when she'd been allowed into Sanctum because there was another name filled in.

William Christopher Daley. Her Dom.

Damn it. She had to stop thinking that way. He wasn't hers. Except he kind of was for the next few weeks. He was hers and he'd written in a couple of lines about monogamy. For the duration of their relationship, they would only sleep together.

Could she really sleep with him? It wasn't that she didn't want to. She totally wanted to. She simply wasn't entirely sure it was a good idea.

She glanced over to where he stood finishing up the dishes. He'd cooked for her, grilling steaks out by the condo pool before bringing her inside for a very cozy dinner where they talked about innocuous things. He told her about his job. She talked about how she'd met her friends. At the end of the meal, he'd given her the contract and told her to read it while he cleaned up. She'd stared at the pages, the words familiar but meaningless since her brain was on the man who wrote them.

They were so different. He could cook. She could barely heat water. She didn't even drink coffee because she found the machines irritating to deal with. He was obviously neat and perfectly organized. She was usually a bit of a mess, her walls peppered with sticky post-it notes containing plot ideas and reminders about her schedule. How could this work?

"Do you have a question about the contract?" He closed the dishwasher door and walked back into his super-neat living room.

He sat down across from her on the love seat and she struggled to form a coherent sentence.

"Do you use the same contract every time?" There. That was semi intelligent.

"I've only signed three contracts. The two prior to this one came before I joined Sanctum. That is a standard Sanctum contract with revisions specifically for the two of us. When I was allowed my membership, I was also allowed use of the contract and the checklists Ian and Alex developed. I keep it on my computer where I do the revisions, and once you've signed it, I'll scan it in and send it back to Ryan. He runs Sanctum for Ian. He keeps a copy of all the contracts. Should we go over your limits?"

The list of hard and soft limits that would let Will know what he could and couldn't do to her. Like flogging and spanking and anal play.

She wrote a lot about anal play, but she'd never cared for it. The one time she'd tried it, it hurt. But she had to wonder if it would be different with a Dom. "I already filled it out."

She'd read the contract. At the end of the day it was simply a document that stated the obvious. She and Will would have sex and she could say no at any time. He could punish her for infractions, but all she had to do to stop it was to use her safe word. He could dominate her but only as long as she let him. It was a consensual relationship but with everything on paper and with a definite time limit.

She picked up the pen and signed the document, handing it back to him.

He took it and laid it aside. "Tell me about your prior relationships."

She frowned. "What about them?"

His brow arched in a way that let her know he was annoyed. "Polite is going to work so much better with me, sweetness. And I would prefer a 'Sir' when you ask me a question or answer one of mine. It's in the contract."

Crap. She hadn't meant to be rude. "Sorry. Sometimes I think my voice comes off as impolite. I wasn't trying to be rude. I was surprised by the question."

His brow rose higher.

"Sir." That shouldn't be so hard to remember.

"I wanted to know about your prior boyfriends. From what I understand, you've never had a D/s relationship."

"Though I do play a sub on TV." Well, she wrote about them.

His lips curved faintly. "I'm serious, Bridget."

That was apparent. He really had that Dommy vibe happening. From the moment he'd let her in his condo, he'd kind of oozed authority. He always seemed in control, but tonight all that willpower was focused on her, and it made her both uncomfortable and a little hot. A lot hot. Her nipples might chafe if they didn't go down soon.

What should she say about her former loves? "They kind of sucked. The relationships that is. I haven't had a ton."

"Of men you would call boyfriends?"

Of men at all, but she nodded anyway. "I had a boyfriend in high school, but he was approved of by my father so I didn't sleep with him."

"Why were you with him if you weren't attracted to him?"

"It was easier than fighting. I needed to keep the peace at home for Amy's sake. There were events to go to that I needed a date for and Nick obliged. We were only friends, but we told people we were dating."

"So you didn't have a real boyfriend at all during high school?"

This was starting to sound like a counseling session, but she was willing to go with it. "No. I didn't fit in at my school. It was a prep school and I always felt out of place. I liked Nick because he didn't fit either. But his father was my dad's lawyer so he was acceptable. No. I didn't have a boyfriend until college and he was unacceptable to say the least."

"Did you care for him?" Will's question sounded more academic than emotional.

"Did I love him? I don't know. I thought so at the time. There was definite lust going on. He was a bad boy on a motorcycle. He was a bartender at this dive off campus. Tall, dark, and handsome. I was crazy about him. Right up until we actually slept together and I realized he didn't believe in anything but getting off as quickly as possible."

"You lost your virginity to this man?" He was so serious, as though he was trying to figure her out.

He should know how simple it had been. "Boy, really. I did. It was awkward and painful, but I thought it would get better. I was with him for about six months and then I found him with one of the waitresses at the bar. But not before I overheard him telling his real girlfriend that I was good for extra cash."

"That must have made you angry."

To say the least. "I spray-painted his motorcycle pink. He wasn't thrilled, but I couldn't care less. I was alone for a while then. I dated some, but I didn't have a serious relationship until Benjy. I lived with him for five years until I finally realized he didn't give a damn about me except that I paid the rent and he could follow his bliss. He was an actor for a while and then he decided to play drums in a band. Yeah, that was successful. Screaming for Georgia. I still don't know what that means. He either really liked Georgia or really hated it. Or maybe Georgia was a girl. People name their kids Georgia, right?"

He utterly ignored her musings. "How did you come to the conclusion he didn't care about you the way he should?"

"Uhm, I ended up in the hospital and he didn't even bother to show up. I don't think he even realized I was there for a few days. I would have had to take a cab home except Chris stayed with me the whole time."

"What were you in the hospital for?" His eyes had narrowed, leaving him looking like a gorgeous hawk scenting prey.

She didn't want to talk about it. She didn't want to talk about that day Serena's ex-husband almost killed her. "It was nothing. A minor incident, but he should have been there."

"It wasn't minor if you were there a few days."

She shrugged. "The point is I knew he wasn't really in love with me. Especially since I later discovered he'd spent the entire time I was in the hospital with his girlfriend. He was hanging around because I would pay for stuff. Story of my life. How about you? When was the last time you were in love?"

His dark head shook. "I don't like that word so I don't use it. I've never been in love. My last relationship was with a woman who was using me as well. Something we have in common."

She should have known a man as seemingly distant as Will wouldn't like the word love. Again, the story of her life. "That's not a good thing to have in common. I think hobbies and a shared love of classical music are more like what we're supposed to look for."

"I don't like classical music. I find it annoying."

"Really? More of a rock guy?" She loved the way his face flushed slightly. He would be so much fun to tease. "Country. Oh, you're a country boy."

"I grew up with it," he conceded. "Why don't you come sit in my lap?"

"Because I have a perfectly good seat where I am." She couldn't help it. It kind of popped out of her mouth. Sarcasm was her default state.

"This isn't going to work if you won't touch me. Now tell me why you don't want to sit in my lap."

She did actually. She wanted to cuddle against him. "I don't know. You don't seem like the type who likes to snuggle."

He thought about that for a moment. "I need affection as much as the next person. And honestly I could say the same of you. You have a hard wall around you. You don't seem like the type of woman who gives affection at all. I suppose I wanted to see if I was wrong."

"I'm affectionate." She was with her friends. She wasn't the type of woman who randomly hugged a stranger. That was more Serena and her friend Avery's specialty. They would find a strange woman crying in the bathroom and suddenly they were her besties while Bridget felt uncomfortable and kind of wanted to leave. When she was upset, she wanted privacy and it seemed best to give others the same.

"You shook hands with Mitch after he flogged you," Will pointed out.

Yes, that had been the slightest bit awkward. "I guess I didn't know protocol for thanking a Dom."

"It depends on the Dom. I would want more than a handshake. I would want you to kiss me. Now I want you to sit on my lap."

Damn it. She was going to do it even if she felt like an idiot. She'd pretty much told this man she would have sex with him. Not pretty much. Had. How was she going to sleep with the man if she didn't touch him? "I'm a little heavy."

His voice was suddenly hard as granite. "Don't even start that shit with me. I don't want to hear what you don't like about yourself. Either get in my lap or we can call it a night and start over again tomorrow."

"Your way or the highway, huh?" That rankled a bit.

"No. If you aren't ready for affection, then I need to say goodnight and go take a cold shower. I'm uncomfortable. If you were uncomfortable in a physical fashion, I would want to take care of you or make it so you could take care of yourself." He stood up and she saw his problem. He had a very large bulge in his jeans.

Really large.

Like epic.

"Wow."

He shrugged. "Yes, it's getting to be obnoxious. I'll see you tomorrow. Perhaps we could have coffee? I have to attend a seminar all afternoon, but my morning is free."

What was she doing? She scrambled to get to her feet as well, feeling weird and awkward but suddenly pretty damn certain she would be making a mistake if she let him show her the door.

He was giving her an out, but she didn't want to take it. She wanted…damn it, she wanted him and she wanted to know what it felt like to really want a man for the first time in her life.

"I had sex because I thought it would get me love. I did it because it was expected in a relationship. I did it because I thought it made me normal and then I turned right around and wrote about the things I wanted in books."

"Did you tell your partners what you wanted?" Will asked.

She laughed at the thought. "Do you know how hard that is? It's one thing to write about it. Hell, I haven't written much D/s anyway. I wrote ménage and I wrote about men who seemed to almost magically get what their partners wanted because that was my fantasy."

"I can't read your mind. No man can. I know it seems like we're idiots, but we don't communicate the same way. We don't react the same way. Even the best meaning man can seem like an insensitive clod if he doesn't understand what you want."

She'd known her share of clods. "It's hard to talk about it."

"It's easier when you're comfortable with the man. When you're comfortable with me, you'll talk."

She shook her head. "But I won't let myself get comfortable with you. Not unless I take the plunge. Can I sit on that thing or will it hurt you?"

"That thing is my penis. It doesn't like being called 'that thing.'" He was awfully cute when offended.

"Does he have a name he does like?" She could come up with a few. Big Boy. Will's Willy. Wonder Willy. Really, she was showing restraint by just grinning inanely.

He sank back into his chair and gave her a shake of his head. "No. I was never one to name my body parts, and go easy on me, but yes, I would love for you to sit here with me."

She'd never sat in a man's lap. She'd had sex, but never simply sat and talked, and suddenly that seemed like a bad thing. Benjy hadn't been big on talking. He'd been big on hopping on top of her, getting off, and then rolling over to go to sleep. When she'd complained, he'd told her she was reading too much of her own work and she shouldn't have such high expectations of a man.

She eased herself onto Will's lap, allowing him to draw her down. Her whole body reacted to the fact that there was a hard cock right under her butt. It was right there and she couldn't help but wiggle to get comfortable.

Will tensed. "Don't."

She stilled in his arms. "I'm sorry. Did that hurt?"

His lips curled up. "It felt far too good, sweetheart, and I really don't want to come in my jeans. Now that I have you here, I have the slightest hope that I might get you into bed, so I'm saving it up."

She wasn't sure why, but that practically made her glow. "You're sure of yourself."

"Nope. That's why I said slightest," Will admitted. "I'm hopeful. Now tell me what you want out of sex. What didn't work with your previous lovers? You said you've never been in a D/s relationship. Did you try at all? Being submissive I mean?"

"I think I'm always somewhat submissive in bed. That might be part of the problem."

"It isn't if your partner understands and knows how to control the situation." His hand was on her leg and she couldn't help but look down at it. Big hands. Strong hands. He used those hands to heal people. What would they feel like on her skin? "You control this, Bridget. If you don't like where my hands are, I'll move them. But I can't know unless you tell me."

"I like them." Perhaps some bravery was called for. "I wasn't thinking about moving them. I was thinking about how they would feel on my bare skin."

He moved his hand up and under her blouse, not too high. He stayed on her waist, but she could feel the heat flowing from him to her. "Relax. This only goes as far as you want it. I want you to want me, Bridget, and not because you're looking for a husband. Not because you think giving yourself to me in bed will manipulate me into doing something."

She stiffened. "I wasn't trying to manipulate them."

"You wanted them to love you. You should know from the get-go that I don't believe in love. Going to bed with me isn't going to get you some romantic drivel from me."

A little of the glow faded. "Fine. You're the one who seems so transactional. What does it buy me?"

"Besides pleasure?"

"I might get that and I might not." History taught her sexual pleasure wasn't worth much.

"I will grant you your skepticism. All right. Going to bed with me buys you my loyalty and commitment for the duration of the contract, and if we end up discovering we enjoy the relationship, then we can renegotiate the contract. I won't sleep around. I won't cheat and I will do my very best to be a good partner to you."

It wasn't romantic. He kind of sucked at that part and she couldn't deny that there was a piece of her that deeply wanted the romantic aspect of a relationship. She wrote romances for a living, but the truth was it was the best offer she'd had in forever. Maybe ever. At least it was honest. "I won't cheat and I'll do my best to be a good partner to you."

His hand tightened on her waist and he sighed as though relieved. "Good. Then come here and kiss me. We'll go slow, but you have to talk to me. You have to tell me what you like and what doesn't feel good. There might be times that I ask you to give something a couple of minutes because it takes a while to get used to the sensation, but you're always in control."

Because he was in control. That was the way it was between a man and woman. It was a primitive thing. He was bigger and stronger and could take what he wanted, but he was in control of those urges in a way none of her previous lovers had been. They hadn't controlled themselves long enough for her to come to real pleasure.

"Tell me what you like." His hand came to the nape of her neck, drawing her mouth to his.

"I like my vibrator." They were so close that their noses touched, a sweet sensation. "It's been my main lover for the last year or so."

"You like a vibe, huh?" He chuckled, and she felt it on her skin as he kissed the bridge of her nose. "I might like to watch you fuck that vibrator.

I might like to watch you fuck in and out of your pussy with it."

"Oh, I like the dirty talk," she admitted because he would find that out soon enough.

"Good because I definitely like to talk dirty. Tell me something, sweetheart. Is your pussy getting wet?" His lips touched hers, just a caress, a brushing of flesh. "Do you think your little pussy is getting ready for me?"

This was so serious because the answer was yes. She was going to start an affair with a man who didn't even believe in love, but there was no going back. She was an adult and her eyes were wide open. Well, they were actually half closed in a kind of aroused daze, but she knew what she was doing. She was going to sleep with Will Daley. "Yes, Sir."

His hips shifted up. "Yeah, that does something for me." His cock was pressed against her backside, his hips moving. "I like the way you say 'Sir.' And I definitely like the way you feel in my arms. Has anyone told you how soft you are, Bridget?"

She wanted to snort and laugh, but he'd caught her and she was somehow under a spell where she forgot to be dismissive and was forced to think about her next words. "No. I don't think I'm soft. I'm hard. I'm a little jagged if you want to know the truth, and I worry I cut people up when I don't really mean to."

His hand closed on her breast. "You are soft. You were born that way, but someone taught you it wasn't okay. I want you to be soft with me. I want you to feel safe enough to be soft around me."

His mouth closed over hers and she let her arms drift around, completely willing to give over to him for the moment.

Chapter Five

Will was going to go insane. Bridget Slaten was going to drive him out of his ever-loving mind if she wiggled that hot ass of hers over his cock again. He pressed his lips to hers and groaned when she opened for him, allowing his tongue to slide against hers in a silky brush.

She tasted like cherries. His brain knew it was likely her lip balm, but he was fairly sure the smell and taste of cherries would always be associated with kissing her, with sliding his hands over her body and finally getting close.

She moved against him, her breasts pressing to his chest as she twisted and turned to allow him access. How could she think she was jagged? Oh, she put on a good show, but he was starting to think it was all an act to cover how soft and sweet she was on the inside.

Their tongues played as he got a feel for her breast. A truly spectacular thing. Real and big and so fucking soft. Softness—that was what he wanted, what he'd been looking for in her. She seemed so brazen on the outside, but he was discovering the sub within, and it did something to him. What if he could take this hellcat and make her purr for him and him alone? He'd always thought he wanted a purely submissive woman, but now he saw the advantages. He wouldn't have to worry about Bridget. She wouldn't let herself be taken for granted. She would likely whack him upside the head if he got too lost in work.

She could be a real partner if he let her.

Was that what he wanted?

He let the thought go because they didn't need anything heavy. Not now. For now they needed to enjoy each other, to find out if they could potentially work.

"I want to see you." He whispered the words against her lips. He could likely have started to ease the clothes off her, but that was too easy. He wanted her to be active. It seemed too much of her sex life had consisted of things that had been done to her. He wanted her with him, not waiting to see what he would do. "Take your clothes off for me."

It was a calculated risk. Despite his belief that she'd likely had a lot of experience, she seemed shy. It could be an act or his instincts could be off. It wouldn't be the first time, but whatever the issue was, he didn't want to lose her. He'd given her an out and if she walked away now he might howl his frustration.

She stopped and he watched as she bit her bottom lip and seemed to come to a decision. She got off his lap, and he hated the loss of her weight, her warmth. She felt right to him in a way other women hadn't. The women he'd dated during college and med school had been all about scratching an itch—for both of them. He'd carefully selected women as ambitious as he was, who wanted no ties. After a few years of his residency, he'd met a friend who took him to a club and he'd figured out why none of his relationships filled his soul. He needed some form of D/s to feel complete.

He'd tried with Starr but even when she curled into his arms, he'd felt the distance between them. He'd thought he could break down her barriers, not understanding the real problems.

Bridget thought she had walls, but the minute she was in his arms, she flowered open for him like a plant in need of sunshine.

He sat back, readjusting his cock as he waited for her.

"I know you don't want to hear about…" she began.

On this he wouldn't move. "You say one thing about your body other than here it is for you, Sir, and I'll show you what my discipline feels like."

She frowned, but even that was cute on her. "Fine, but I would have warned you."

Almost defiantly, she pulled her shirt over her head and quickly had her bra undone. Her breasts bounced free and she went to work on her jeans. She shoved those off and got rid of her panties, too. She put her arms out to her sides. "Here it is for you, Sir."

Such a bitch. He was surprised to find he didn't mind it.

He stared at her for a moment, taking her in. There was no way to miss the surgical scar on her abdomen and he wondered if that was one of the things she'd been planning on warning him about. His first instinct was to study it because it told a tale. She'd either been in an accident of some kind or someone had tried to hurt her. She'd likely lost her spleen. Not serious? That was pretty damn serious. But he was going to let it go for now. He was going to focus on all the beauty in front of him and not something that would likely remind her of a bad time.

She was scared he would reject her and so she put up a front. Some Doms would spank her, but he had other plans. A spanking would just get her hot, and he actually wanted to teach her something.

"Touch your breasts. Hold them up for me."

She frowned as though that was the last thing she'd expected to hear from him. "Because they practically hit the floor?"

Or he could throw a spanking in, too. "I'm giving you one last warning and then it's ten for every nasty word that comes out of your mouth about yourself. Hold them up for me because they're like ripe fruit and I want you to offer them to me. Did my erection wilt at the sight of your body? Did I faint dead away and beg out of the contract? Or did my mouth water the minute I laid eyes on those tits?"

"I'm guessing it was the mouth watering thingee."

"See, I knew you were smart, sweetheart."

Slowly her hands came up and all the defiance seemed to have fled. She turned the loveliest shade of pink, as though she'd finally realized she was naked in front of him and he was enjoying the view.

"You have the prettiest nipples," he said, watching her. "I'm going to suck on them soon." There was no way he could miss the flush that covered her skin. She liked the idea. "Is that what you want? Do you want me to suck on your nipples? I'll lick them and nibble on them and make sure they're round and hard by the time I'm done."

"Can I quote you on that?"

The last thing he wanted was to get turned into a hero for one of her books, but as long as she kept it to sex, he didn't see a problem with it. "Sure. Do you often quote your lovers in your books?"

The thought made him uneasy, but he tried to let it go. The idea of Bridget fucking to get material kind of made him want to lose his damn mind, but he didn't have a right to judge.

The brat was back. Her chocolate eyes rolled. "Uhm, I think Benjy's version of dirty talk was 'do you wanna fuck, babe?' That was about it. Not a lot of conversation there."

And yet she'd stayed with him for years. "Come back to my lap now."

She nearly stumbled in her haste to move. Yeah, that did something for him, too. He was self-aware enough to know that Bridget's desire for him soothed his aching ego.

She stopped before him and a grimace swept across her face. "I'm a little messy."

That got him to sit up. He'd been joking about her pussy being wet. He'd barely touched her. He'd expected to do much more before he got her all ripe and ready to fuck. She started to take a step back. He reached out and caught her waist, stopping her. "Don't move."

He leaned over and took a deep breath. Fuck. She wasn't kidding. He could smell her arousal, and it did all sorts of things to his cock. The bastard was practically thumping against his jeans, trying to get out. He'd let his dick make the decision to sign the contract with Bridget, but it was going to have to be patient because he intended to seal this particular deal in his own way. He was going to bring her as much pleasure as he could, to show her what it would mean to be his sub.

"You smell good. Perfect." He put his nose right in the middle of her labia, rubbing it in so he wouldn't lose her scent. She responded so fucking fast. He'd never had a woman get so damn wet from as little as a kiss and some dirty talk.

"You're a doctor. Isn't that a bit unhygienic. I mean, I write about it and stuff because…oh, god, that feels good…but isn't it…doesn't it bother you?"

It didn't bother him at all. It fucking turned him on. Insanely. He suddenly couldn't wait to taste her. "This is a perfectly beautiful and normal pussy. You have my word on it. In my expert opinion, this is the most perfect pussy I've ever seen."

He licked her, reveling in the taste of her arousal. He sucked on one side of her labia and then the other. Licking and sucking her like she was the ripest piece of fruit he'd ever tasted.

"Oh, my god." Bridget's hands came down on his shoulders as though she needed some balance to stay upright. Her breath came out in little pants. "I'm taking that with a grain of salt, Doc. You're a brain guy not an obstetrician."

But suddenly brains had nothing on the piece of anatomy in front of him. He gave her a long lick, parting her and finding the pearly nub of her clitoris. Her brain would process the pleasure, nerve endings sending messages along her spine, but it would all start with that button. "Spread your legs, Bridget."

For once she didn't argue with him. She moved, spreading her legs and finding a wider stance. He pulled back the hood and completely exposed her clit.

His cock wasn't going to wait much longer. If he played with her for too long, he would likely come in his jeans and he didn't want that. He wanted to be buried deep inside her. He had to give her what she needed so he could find his own satisfaction.

"Do you like this?" He used one hand to hold back the hood of her clit and the other to explore her pussy. With a single finger, he started to gently fuck her as he blew on her clit, letting her feel the heat of his mouth.

"Yes, oh god, yes." Her legs were trembling, but she held strong.

"Sir, Bridget. You call me Sir when I'm fucking you." Oh, she was tight. Her pussy was tight as a drum. How long had it really been for her? She was going to strangle his cock.

"Yes, Sir. Yes, I like it. Oh, Sir, please. Please." Her muscles tightened around his finger as though trying to keep him inside, as though that single finger could ever be enough for her.

He would give her more, but not until she screamed for him. "Please what, sweetheart?"

He loved the desperation in her voice. "Please lick my clit. Please. Sir, it would feel so good. It's been so long since I was touched there, and I think you'll do it better than anything I've ever had before. Please lick it."

Well, when she put it like that, how could he possibly refuse? She was so unashamed, so open that it made him want to give her everything he had. As he gave her another finger, fucking deep inside, he took her clit

68

between his lips and sucked. Hard.

Bridget screamed. Her whole body shook and he could feel his fingers get coated in her arousal. She came all over his hand.

Bridget coming was the hottest thing he'd ever experienced in his life.

He couldn't stand it a second longer. He pulled his hand out and stood, immediately bending to catch her as she slumped over. He lifted her easily and made his way to the bedroom. He kicked open the door, deposited her on the bed, and started to shove his clothes off.

"That was amazing." She looked up at him with sleepy eyes. "Seriously, better than a vibrator."

He was glad he ranked higher than the inanimate object, but he had better things to do than bask in the glow of her praise. He opened the nightstand drawer and grabbed a condom.

"Wait," Bridget said, getting to her knees.

Fuck. She was going to bail on him and he would likely drop to the floor and beg her. He was kind of at that stage. He needed her. Damn it. "You want to leave?"

"No. I want to see you. You got to see me. Can I touch it?"

His cock? She wasn't leaving. She wanted to touch him, to see him. He stood in front of her and nodded, though he knew it was a mistake. "Touch me, sweetheart."

She stared at him, her eyes wide, and he suddenly knew what it meant to feel twelve feet tall. She was looking at him like he was an ice cream cone and she couldn't wait to lick him up. His cock pulsed at the thought.

She moved to the end of the bed, and her fingers brushed against his cock, making it twitch. "You like that?"

So she thought turnabout was fair play? He pulled in a shaky breath. "Yes, I did. I'll always like your hand wrapped around my dick. I'd like your mouth there, too, but I'm afraid I'll come too soon."

Her lips curled up and she sank to her knees on the floor. "Then you'll have to find a way to get hard again, won't you?"

As her lips found the head of his dick, he knew he'd been right. She was going to drive him mad.

* * * *

He was gorgeous in a pair of leathers, but out of them he'd moved into Greek god territory. She wasn't sure what she was doing, but some inner vixen had taken over and she suddenly didn't care. With her whole body still humming from the orgasm Will had given her, Bridget was ready for some payback.

He stood in front of her, all six feet three inches of purely chiseled male. He really would look good on one of her covers, but she didn't want other women seeing him like this. Who would be able to resist? Broad shoulders and a muscled chest and perfectly shaped abs. She let her fingers find the skin of his hips. So soft. Soft skin covering steel.

And his cock. A true thing of beauty. There was already a drop of pre-come on the slit. He'd tasted her. He'd put his tongue right on her and drawn on her cunt like she made nectar there. It wasn't like she'd never had a guy go down on her, but before it had been a rote thing. Like something he had to quickly check off a list in order to move on to bigger and better things. A quick lick. A tiny suck and then she found herself spread and penetrated and oops, it was over.

Not Will Daley. No. He liked to play and take his time and she believed in a clean balance sheet.

She dragged her tongue over the head of his cock.

"Hold it. Wrap your hand around it and hold it still." Will hissed a little as she licked him again.

Power. She felt it rush through her. This big strong man was practically trembling. She could make him feel as good as he'd made her feel. Somehow being on her knees in front of him gave her power she'd never felt before.

He would appreciate it. He wouldn't see her laving affection on his cock as his due. He would tell her how he wanted it and praise her when she was done.

Damn it. She really was a sub. She'd kind of hoped this wouldn't work for her because all the "Sirs" and "Masters" got to her from time to time, but something had settled deep inside her.

Of course she only had him for a while.

She shoved that thought aside. She was living in the moment. That was where she always made her mistake. She reached for too much, wanted a stability no one could give her. Not really. Marriages didn't have to be forever—most weren't. Even some that lasted weren't happy. What Will was offering her was honest.

And there was zero doubt that she wanted him.

She licked his cockhead. Long and thick, she could barely close her fingers around the stalk of his dick. She pumped as she drew the head inside her mouth, tasting the salt that dripped from the slit of his cock.

"That feels like heaven." His hand found her hair and sank in. "You are awfully good at that, sweetheart."

It was odd how those few words made her feel. Giving good head probably wasn't something she wanted engraved on a plaque and mounted to her wall, but the knowledge that he liked what she was doing to him filled her with a need to do more. She could be good at this. They could be good together.

In bed. She had to remember to keep it to the bedroom.

She let her eyes drift up and saw Will watching. He was such a gorgeous beast of a man, with his dark eyes staring at the place where his cock sank inside her mouth.

"Take more."

She took more. She worked slowly, methodically, not wanting to miss an inch of him. Though he was big, she was certain she could take him. In her mouth. In her pussy. Hell, the way she felt now she was ready to let him into her ass. Sex was different with him, better. She felt better.

"Cup my balls." He was a bossy sort but then that was probably why he'd gone into the whole Dom thing.

She sucked and licked while she moved her hand to fondle his balls. The good doc obviously believed in a careful grooming routine, and she was so freaking happy she'd shaved before coming over here. She'd thought about him and carefully shaved her pussy, the optimist in her making a showing for once.

Will's hands tightened in her hair, pulling at her. Even that sharpness felt good. He pulled her off his cock. "I can't take anymore. I don't want to come in your mouth, Bridget. I want to get inside. Let me get inside you."

She got back on the bed, her hands shaking slightly. He was going to do it. He was going to roll a condom on and fuck her. She was going to be his for the night. He was going to be hers. Her third lover.

"Bridget? Are you afraid of me?"

She looked up to find him looming over her. His cock was erect, straining her way, and he'd rolled the condom on. Everything was ready except her heart. "I'm not afraid. I'm not. It's just…it's not as casual as I thought it would be."

If he fucked her it would mean something to her. She could say it didn't, but her soul would know.

He nodded and for a moment she thought he was going to turn and walk away. Fear seized her. She shouldn't have said anything. Her big mouth always got her in trouble. Now it was going to cost her the weeks she could have spent with him.

"It's not casual." He climbed on the bed, spreading her legs wide. "Sweetheart, I can't promise you forever, but I can tell you that the way I feel right now is not a casual thing."

She would take it. It might not last forever, but she could have him now.

He settled between her legs, the heat of his body flowing over her. She loved the way his weight felt as he lowered his mouth down to cover her own.

He kissed her as she felt his cock at the entrance of her pussy. "I'll take care of you, sweetheart. While we're together, let me take care of you."

He kissed her again and she finally decided on a word. She'd been trying to find a word to describe how it felt when he kissed her. Hot. Aroused. They were there, but didn't even begin to cover it.

Cherished. When he kissed her, she felt cherished.

"You feel so good." He groaned against her mouth.

He pressed in, his cock invading and stretching her but in the most pleasant way.

He went up on his elbows, taking some of the weight off her. "Wrap your legs around me. I want to feel you around me."

She hooked her legs around his waist and gasped as he gained another inch. His eyes were closed as he worked methodically, gently pressing in and pulling out. He was so careful it was driving her insane.

And then he was in. His cock filled her to bursting but she wouldn't change anything. She tilted her hips up, trying to take more.

"Like I said before, you're so fucking soft," he said, looking down at her. "Keep your eyes on me. I want to watch. I couldn't see you come before."

He pushed in, twisting his hips in a way that let his pelvis grind against her clitoris.

She couldn't breathe. It was starting again. Orgasms before had been small things. They'd been pleasant when she managed one, but Will's tongue had taken her to an entirely different level. He seemed intent on proving he could manage the same thing with his cock.

Over and over he fucked deep inside, his body working hers while he held her eyes. When she started to close them he would remind her, forcing her into an intimacy she'd never known before. Her previous lovers hadn't cared whether she'd come or not, much less wanted to watch her while she did it.

He hit some magic spot deep inside and she couldn't help but moan.

He grinned, the expression making him look younger, less grim than his normal serious look. "There it is. Yeah, now I've got you, sweetheart. Try to hold me off now."

She wasn't trying to do anything except breathe because he pressed in again and her body went off like a bomb. Pure pleasure sparked through her, racing through her veins and making her call out his name over and over. She tightened her legs, wanting the moment to last. She was fairly certain she left claw marks on his back, but he didn't seem to mind. He picked up the pace, slamming into her and sending her into a second wave.

His whole body stiffened as he rode out his orgasm, finally falling on top of her.

The world seemed hazy and she was fairly certain she was drunk on lust or whatever he wanted to call it.

Affection. He'd said he needed affection. She let her arms wrap around him, holding him close. He didn't shove off her to go to the bathroom or turn over to go to sleep. He laid his head on her chest, one hand on her breast, and they lay together for the longest time before sleep finally took her.

Chapter Six

"You did what?" Serena asked as she patted baby Tristan's back and paced the floor. Her eyes narrowed as she looked Bridget over. "Tell me you're joking."

They'd traded their margarita lunches for afternoons at either Bridget's or Chris's place since Serena had given birth. Her son was kind of the cutest thing in the world. Well, he definitely won in the baby category. Bridget thought back to the morning before when she'd slipped out of Will's condo before he woke up. The sheet had slipped and she'd gotten a spectacular view of his ass. It was a superlative male specimen and she'd wondered how many squats the man had to do to achieve it.

"She's not joking." Chris shook his head at her with a sigh. "She really ran away like a cowardly rabbit."

Bridget put the tray of crackers and cheese she'd bought at the market out on the table with a thud. "It was not cowardly. It was a strategic withdrawal."

"It was a massive mistake since your butt is going to feel that at some point in time." Serena placed Tristan in the bouncy seat and strapped him in. The baby immediately started kicking his legs and batting at the toys dangling above him with a delighted glee. His mother wasn't so amused. She turned to Bridget. "Did he give you permission to leave?"

"I don't need permission to leave." She was a freaking grown-up.

Serena's head shook. "You signed a contract. I assure you there was something in there about leaving, unless Master Will is a total pushover and I hadn't heard he was."

Something about the way she said it got to Bridget. Serena had the perfect life. Two gorgeous men, a sweet baby boy, career to die for, and she didn't even do her own laundry. "Well, I guess the perfect princess doesn't know everything, does she?"

Serena's jaw dropped and she pointed her index finger Bridget's way. "You do not want to go there. I've done nothing to deserve that. You're the one who's taking a good thing and tossing it away."

She was the fuck-up. Again. "Is that what I'm doing? So because I won't bow and scrape to some Dom, I'm ruining everything."

Serena's finger wagged. "You stop this instant. We are not having this fight. You think about it for two seconds. You can't sign a contract with a man and then bail on him and expect everything to be great the next day. This is what you do, Bridge. This is how things go wrong for you."

Bridget took a step back, her anger deflating because she was pretty sure Serena was right. Younger Bridget would have told Wiser Serena to bite her ass and never talked to her again, but Older Bridget really loved her friends. "Wow, your mom finger is strong today. It's all full of judgmental righteousness."

Serena backed down, a flush staining her face pink. "Sorry. It comes naturally now."

"Let the hormones flow, ladies. I think I'll take Tristan and we'll run away. Let's run from all the scary estrogen, baby boy." Chris had taken a seat by the baby as if to ward off all the bad vibes coming from the women.

What the hell was she doing? She was fighting with her best friend because she felt stupid? She had to get over this shit. "I'm sorry, Serena. I'm feeling weird about Will and I'm taking it out on you."

"Look at Auntie Bridget. She's pulled on her big girl panties," Chris cooed to the baby.

She wasn't that mature. "Dude, I can still take you out."

Serena held up her hands. "Everyone stop and let's figure this out.

Bridget, why did you leave Will and how has he handled it?"

"Serena is skipping the good parts. No starting in the middle. I want the whole shebang. And by shebang I mean the banging. How was the good doctor in bed?" Chris asked.

Heavenly. Perfect. "Okay."

They both stared at her.

She could feel herself blushing. "Fine. He was amazing. It was totally vanilla and it was still the best sex I've ever had. Are you happy now?"

"Mostly." Serena sat down and took a sip of her iced tea. They were supposed to be talking plots and promo for their next books, but it never turned out that way. They tended to gossip about what was happening at Sanctum and about Serena's and Chris's sex lives. "He treated you well?"

She nodded. "He didn't even mention my scars. He was dirty and nasty and he took care of me in a way that made me pretty much want to drop to my knees and beg him to love me. And yes, that was why I ran like a scared little girl." She slumped into her chair, shaking her head. "It was so embarrassing. I woke up next to this god of a man and all I could think was 'please don't let him see me in the cold light of day.'"

"Oh, she's so getting her ass spanked," Chris said with wide eyes. "How did he handle it? Did he come storming over that morning? This was yesterday, right?"

Yep. A whole day and a half had passed since she'd last seen Will. "He didn't. Come over, that is. He didn't even knock on the door on his way to work." She shrugged. "I guess I pissed him off or something."

Or he'd had enough of her and he was grateful to have avoided the next morning's scene.

She'd gone to bed the night before wondering where he was but too afraid and embarrassed to knock on his door. God, she'd screwed up again.

"So, I need a new date to my sister's wedding," she said with a fake smile on her face. "I'm down to strippers. Get me a good one, Chris. But not the dude who humps the pole. He scares me."

"Oh, honey, you have to talk to Will." Serena leaned over. "You can't slip out of his bed and then avoid him for the rest of your life."

Actually she could. If she left now and then paid someone to clean out her condo, she could move to another city, change her name, her hair color, and live a Will-free life with lots and lots of cats. The virtual kind. Maybe houseplants could be her thing. Unless she killed them all. Fish.

They were easy, right?

"And you can't move to another city and get some unnamed house pet," Chris said.

Well, at least he knew her really well. One guy in the world knew the real her and loved her, and naturally it was the dude who didn't like vaginas.

There was a thought…

"You're not becoming a lesbian, either," Serena said.

"If I did, I would totally be into you." Somehow, her life wasn't quite as heartbreaking when she shared her problems with these two.

A smile lit up Serena's face. "Back at you. Now let's figure out how you're going to handle the man you are actually attracted to because he seems to be throwing a hissy fit of his own."

Her heart dropped. "He's not throwing a fit. That doesn't seem like Will. He's figured out that he's not that interested. Now that I think about it, I guess this whole thing really was kind of a test run. I mean the contract was only for two weeks anyway. I think the sex wasn't as good for him."

Chris groaned. "We have got to work on your self-esteem. Can I see your contract?"

"Oh, I think I left it at his place. I was kind of in a hurry to get out. I was lucky it was early in the morning because I didn't bother to put on my shirt. He rolled over and I ran. I think I left my undies behind, too. Very classy of me." What had she been so afraid of? Everything. It had been too intimate, too much. She'd felt too much and not knowing how he felt made her anxious. He might have felt nothing at all.

He'd probably had hundreds of women, and she was fairly certain she wouldn't measure up. Her sex life had been boring for a woman who wrote about crazy bondage sex with up to six guys. It had taken them a while to figure out where to put hottie number six. The first five had been easy. Pussy, ass, mouth, and two hands. But that sixth had been a challenge. About two bottles of wine in, Chris had come up with boobs. Yeah, she'd been lucky her heroine wasn't claustrophobic.

"And he hasn't called or texted?" Serena asked.

"Nope." She'd gotten nothing. She'd heard his door slam at eleven a.m. the day before and nothing from him since. She wasn't going to admit to sitting and waiting for sounds from the hallway. She definitely wasn't going to admit that she'd spied out her peephole at every creak of the floor. All she'd gotten to see was Mrs. Hannigan wheeling her groceries in and that girl old man Mussey said was his daughter, but Bridget really knew was a hooker because of her shoes. And the fact that she looked absolutely nothing like Mr. Mussey. And the fact that she'd watched the chick counting her cash one day. Bridget was fairly certain she overcharged since the "visits" never lasted more than twenty or thirty minutes.

She was totally going to end up like Mr. Mussey, hiring call boys so she had some kind of human connection. She wouldn't even be able to say it was her son since she was never going to get married. She would have to call him her nephew or something. How pathetic. She couldn't even get her future hooker right.

"Did we lose her?" Chris asked.

"She's figuring out how dire her situation is." Serena snapped her fingers. "Come out of the pity party. Here's what you're going to do. First, you're going to write a letter of apology to your Dom for fleeing the scene of the crime. Then you're going to make him dinner."

"So you think I should kill him." It would be an interesting way out of her embarrassment.

Serena huffed. "Brat. You can cook a little. You make a very nice enchilada bake. Do that and bake your chocolate chip cookies. Then you serve it to him naked."

Chris gave the plan a thumbs-up. "All the easier for him to spank you, my dear. Because that is very likely happening."

"It won't save you, but it might—and I say might—put him in a better mood when he gets to the spanking part. So the sex was vanilla?" Serena asked.

There hadn't been a particular kink to it, but something about the way Will had forced her to look into his eyes, made her talk about the sex, had been…a revelation. "It was intense. No bondage or spanking, but it was intense. It was like I couldn't breathe without him. That sounds stupid, but for those few moments, I felt connected to him in a way I never have before."

Serena pointed her way. "And that, my dear, is why you ran."

Shit. She'd gotten scared and she'd run away so she wouldn't have to face the fact that the next morning would have been a letdown. Or that he hadn't felt the same, that it had all been one sided.

"I don't know that it matters now." His silence was answer enough. If he'd wanted to talk, even to yell at her, he would have shown up on her doorstep. Hell, she hadn't even warranted a text telling her it had been nice, but see ya later, baby.

There was a knock on the door. A pounding really.

"Are you expecting someone?" Chris asked, getting to his feet. Despite his status as a big ol' bottom, he tended to be very take-charge when his Dom wasn't around and they were all alone. It probably had something to do with him having to watch she and Serena almost die once.

"No." She let Chris do his thing. The building had a security guard, but it made Chris feel better to answer the door.

He stalked over and looked out the peephole. "Shit. Serena, I believe our afternoon is over. Get Tristan ready and I'll take you home. Bridget, this one is for you."

She stood. "Of course, it's for me. It's my condo."

She threw open the door because Chris would have told her if it was someone scary.

Except he hadn't.

Will stood in the doorway, his eyes red and his normally perfect clothes wrinkled. There was a scowl on his face and he held up her contract. "Did you bother to read this? Or did it mean so little to you that you left it behind along with your underwear. I threw those away since I amended our contract and you are no longer allowed the privilege of wearing them."

She had to stop her jaw from dropping. "What? You amended our contract? Can you do that?" She looked back at Chris. "Can he do that?"

Chris shrugged as he picked up Tristan's baby bag, obviously eager to make his getaway. "He's the Dom. I think he can do most of what he wants."

Will walked inside, not bothering to wait for an invitation. "Ah, you're having a party. Tell me. Did this party start yesterday morning? Is that why I woke up and my sub was nowhere to be found? I amended that part of the contract, too. I thought it would be obvious that when we spend the night fucking like jackrabbits, you're supposed to be there in the morning."

"Dude, company." She could feel herself blush.

"Oh, sweetheart, if you didn't want to have this argument in public, you shouldn't have had people over. I am tired. I haven't slept in over twenty-four hours so I am incapable of being polite." He slapped the contract on her breakfast bar. "And don't you dare dude me again."

"Will, it was good to see you. Don't be too hard on her. She's smart about so many things. This is not one of them." Serena winked her way as she made her exit.

"Talk to you later." Chris gave her the universal signal for call me later.

And they were gone. And they called her a coward.

"Why have you been awake for twenty-four hours?"

He glanced down at his watch. "Twenty-nine hours. I had one of those days. And nights. ER got slammed. Big accident on 75. Twenty-car pileup. Lots of head trauma. Then when I thought I could come home, some idiot decided to skateboard without a helmet. You know those flips they like to do? He didn't quite get it right. Surprisingly enough the concrete was harder than his head."

So he had a good reason he hadn't come over. "Whoa. Is he okay?"

"I don't know. I had to remove a portion of his skull. I can't do anything until the swelling goes down. I've probably got a day or two before I have to decide. I intend to spend those days pounding your ass."

Now that they were alone and she really looked at him, she realized she wasn't afraid of him in any way except the obvious. He might break her heart, but he wouldn't hurt her. She relaxed a bit because he was here and that meant it wasn't over. "In an anal sex way? Or in a spanking way? You'll have to be more specific because my brain can't differentiate."

He ran a hand through his hair. "In a spanking way. Damn it, Bridget. Why did you run?"

"I don't know. I didn't know if I was supposed to stay or go. I got confused."

"Which is why the contract now states that you stay. And you owe me thirty smacks. I'm going to the bathroom. When I come back out, you better be ready."

She shook her head. "You can't punish me for something I didn't know about."

"Watch me," he said as he turned away. "It was common sense. There is a clause in our contract about common sense. I'm invoking it."

"Use my bathroom. It's down the hall. I don't know if I put soap in the guest bathroom." She never used it.

"Fine." He strode away.

And she stood there because of all the reactions, she hadn't expected this one. He was pissed. Seriously pissed. He was upset because she hadn't been there when he woke up.

How should she handle him? She wasn't afraid of the spanking. She'd been spanked before. Even the hard smacks did something for her. She was comfortable with her freakiness. If he spanked her hard, she would have an excuse to cry and she really needed to cry. She could cry and he could feel in control.

All in all it was a good plan.

Now she knew. He wanted her in bed when he woke up. She glanced down at the contract. Will didn't believe in love, but he believed in that stupid contract. He cared enough to amend it.

He was taking a while. She walked into her bedroom.

There he was. He'd lain down on her bed as if he couldn't move another muscle. He was still dressed, still in his shoes. With his eyes closed and his arms at his side, he looked like an exhausted boy. A beautiful, tired boy. Her guy. For now.

How should she handle him?

He'd taken care of her. Maybe it was time someone took care of him. She wasn't sure she would be good at it, but she was going to try. She carefully eased his shoes off and found a blanket to put over him.

"Don't think I've forgotten about the spanking." His eyes didn't open.

"I wouldn't dream of it, Doc." There was something about seeing him in her girlie room that made her smile. Her bedspread was a pretty silver and she'd indulged in a bunch of eggplant-colored pillows to contrast. It gave the whole place a glamorous feel. Will looked like a sleepy predator.

"Shitty day. Shitty, shitty day," he murmured. "Kiss me."

He was going to kill her. She leaned over and brushed her lips against his. He sighed and his breathing became even, sleep taking him.

She was already in love with him because she was an idiot. She was a stupid fool who didn't know when to protect herself, but it didn't matter.

She had a little time to prove to him that it could work.

Damn, she hoped she still had the recipe for those enchiladas.

* * * *

Will yawned as he moved from the bedroom to the living room and wondered exactly how much he'd fucked up. When he'd woken up the day before and found himself alone in bed, he'd thought about how to handle Bridget. She'd run. He hadn't expected that and he really should have.

He just hadn't figured out if she was bored or skittish.

"Damn it." Bridget's voice carried down the hall.

Why had he fallen asleep in her bed? He never slept anywhere except his own place. He made sure to take women to his place. Always. But he'd walked toward her bathroom and her bed had looked so inviting. He'd lain down because he kind of wanted to see what type of mattress she liked. It was one of the mattresses that conformed to a person's body and he'd sunk into it like he'd found paradise. The bed had smelled like her—all sharp and citrusy, with the hint of sweet cherries.

He'd had a crappy day and all he'd wanted to do was sleep and be surrounded by that scent.

But he was awake now and he had to deal with the fact that he'd lost his cool.

He never did that. He was always in control around his lovers. He never barged in and caused some stupid scene. He was the anti-drama guy.

She was standing over the stove as he walked into the room. She bent over, giving him a spectacular view of her ass. Her hair flowed down her back. He caught sight of bare skin and wondered if she was wearing a crop top.

"Bridget?"

She stood up, her back stiffening, and then stopped.

Damn it. He was going to have to apologize. "I need to talk to you."

She turned around and he damn near had a heart attack. She wasn't wearing a shirt at all. She stared at him for a second. "I made dinner."

He'd been pretty sure she didn't cook. "Really?"

One hand went on her hip and she gave him the sassiest frown. "Yes, really. I can manage to follow a recipe. Sort of. It should be edible."

She'd cooked and she'd foregone her shirt. It was definitely a good sign. Maybe he hadn't fucked up. Maybe she was more into the D/s relationship than he'd thought she was.

"It smells wonderful, sweetheart. And you look stunning."

She blushed. "Serena told me being naked might make you less annoyed with the fact that I ran away."

His affection for Bridget's best friend rose. His cock was already erect and he had to admit, she had every bit of his attention. Usually his brain was working on ten different things, but when he was with Bridget, he was focused. He couldn't think of anything but her. She was a challenge.

"Tell me why you ran."

"The boobs aren't enough?" She was a bit insecure and he couldn't figure that out. She was fucking gorgeous.

"The boobs are lovely, but you're not getting out of punishment." Now that he knew she was all right, he wanted to spank that sweet ass of hers. His hand was itching and his cock was twitching. She got his motor running.

It couldn't last. He would want peace eventually. This crazy focus on her made him feel so fucking good though. It had been forever—maybe never—since he was so focused on a woman.

Her shoulders squared. "Fine. It was silly of me. I should have woken you up and told you I was leaving. I get it. I was a little childish. I can handle a spanking. I kind of like them. Then we can have dinner. If you want to."

"I want to. How long does it need to cook?" He didn't want to screw up her dinner plans. She'd bent for him and he was willing to bend for her.

"It's got another thirty minutes. It might be really bad. I usually order takeout or nuke a dinner or something. This feels weird. The naked thing feels weird. Maybe it's because you're all dressed and my boobs are hanging out."

"Well, maybe you would feel better if you were actually naked. Take off the pants. You don't need clothes when we're alone. Do your characters wear clothes around their Doms?"

"No, but I have to admit that apparently my characters are more carefree than I am."

"You wanted some experience." An idea was brewing in his head. "Let's try living as a D/s couple until after your sister's wedding. You'll get real world experience out of it."

"What do you get out of it?"

"I get to fuck the hell out of you for a couple of weeks. I get to spank you and discipline you. Don't think this is charity here. I want you, Bridget." Maybe after a couple of weeks, he could think straight again. Maybe if he fucked her out of his system, he would be able to concentrate on something other than her.

Her hands went to the waistband of her sweat pants and she slowly pushed them over and off her hips. "Look at me. No undies. See, I can obey. Also, I haven't done laundry lately. I'm not the world's greatest housekeeper."

"Give it to me and I'll throw yours in with mine. Now come here and let me look at you. God, you're the fucking best thing I've seen since the last time I saw you." She made his mouth water. He sank down on her couch. It was a good height for what he intended to do. He'd kept it vanilla up to this point, but it was time to put them on a proper footing.

She walked across the space, the tiniest awkwardness showing through, but he knew she would get accustomed to being naked. After a few days, he hoped she would come to enjoy it. "You want to do my laundry? I kind of thought you would order me to do yours."

"If I want a maid, I'll hire one. I've seen your bathroom. I would not hire you." She was a little messy. He could live with it, though he intended to introduce her to his maid. She came twice a week and was worth every penny. Bridget stopped in front of him and he took in her form, allowing his eyes to enjoy for a moment. "No, beautiful, I don't mind doing your laundry with mine. Every D/s couple is different. We need to find our strengths and play to them and find our weaknesses and figure out how to balance. Poor baby. It looks like some man left his mark."

He reached up and touched her left breast. There was a small hematoma from where he'd sucked on her skin too hard. He needed to remember that she was very fair and would bruise easily.

She looked down. "Oh, I didn't even notice that. It's okay. I think I probably did a number on your back."

He leaned over and kissed the spot. "I didn't notice that either until I got to work and changed into scrubs and Jameson from Peds asked if I'd tangled with a wildcat. Don't move."

She was short, petite he should say. Standing in front of him, he could easily lean over and suck a pretty pink nipple into his mouth. He let his lips touch that velvety skin before very gently suckling on the bud. He could take his time. He wasn't on call. He had all night and he intended to revel in her.

It had been a brilliant plan. Moving past the academic and into the real Dom sub relationship. It was only for a little while, but he could blow past all the bullshit and get to where he wanted to go which was straight to bed, though he intended to prove he was far more creative than a man who needed a bed to get it on.

She was his for the next few weeks. He was a man who didn't like to dwell on the past, and the future was pretty much set. He worked. He studied so he could work more. But the now, oh, the now, included the complex and gorgeous woman who had just handed herself over to him.

She was his to fuck and spank and please and yes, he even liked the idea of doing her laundry with his. He liked the idea that he would have someone to watch over and take care of for a while. Not someone. Her.

"All right. Let's get the hard part over with. Over my lap." He sat back, enjoying how flushed she'd gotten from him playing with her nipples. No woman had ever responded to him quite as fast or perfectly as Bridget did.

Maybe the hard part could be the fun part, too. He really didn't want to wait and there was no reason to. He could smell her from where he was sitting. He could see her pussy. She was already ripe.

He stood up. Hell, he didn't need clothes when they were alone either.

"I can't get over your lap if you're standing up. Your lap disappears." Her logic was impeccable.

"Brat. You'll get your spanking, but you're going to ride my cock while you do it. It's a game. We'll see if I can get all thirty licks in before I explode." There was another thing he wanted to talk to her about. He kicked his jeans off and pulled his shirt over his head. "Bridget, I'm clean. You know Sanctum requires medical tests and I use condoms for casual affairs."

"I thought this was casual."

How did he get her to understand? She seemed to want something from him and he wasn't sure what that thing was. "I told you it's not. I'm going to be monogamous during our contract. I can go across the hall and grab some condoms. Unless you have some here."

She shook her head. "No. I don't have any and it's fine. I took all my tests and I'm on the pill. I know Big Tag is hard on the single guys."

He made them test once a month during their probationary period. Will didn't mind. Tag took his club seriously and Will admired that. He'd been to too many places where no one gave a shit. "He wants to make sure everyone's safe."

"So it's okay. I'm protected. You're clean. We're both going to be faithful during our fling. Let's play, Sir." She was staring at his cock, looking like she could eat him up.

He kissed her. He hadn't meant to. He meant for this to be hard and fast and satisfying. This encounter was supposed to prove to her that he was the Master and she was the sub. But he couldn't resist worshipping that mouth of hers. He dove in, letting his tongue slide against hers because she immediately flowered open for him. His hands delved into the silk of her hair and he brought their bodies together. Yeah, he liked being naked with her. He liked how soft she was against him and he couldn't feel her properly with a layer of clothing between them. He couldn't feel the hard nubs of her nipples against his chest, couldn't rub his cock against the soft curve of her belly.

He broke off the kiss and pulled her close, hugging her tight to him. "You won't regret it."

Her arms came around his waist. "I'm sure I will, but I don't want to back out, Sir. I want to be your sub for a while."

Then it was time to show her what that meant. He sank back down on her couch, spreading his legs. "Come here. Take me."

His cock was about as hard as it could get. The damn thing pointed straight up, practically begging her for attention.

"I don't know how this is punishment, Will. And I'm in control." She started to straddle him.

Oh, she thought she knew how this would go, did she? It was going to be fun to prove her wrong. "You think because you're on top that you're in control?" He could feel the heat of her pussy hovering over his cock. "You think you can torture me with that sweet cunt of yours? Let me prove to you that I don't need to be on top to top you."

He wrapped his hands around her hips and pressed up, filling her in one hard thrust. She was tight, but she was also wet. She could take him, but he bet she'd planned on taking him slowly. That was not how this would go.

"Oh, my god," Bridget breathed. Her body flushed with arousal as he held her hard against his cock. "You're so damn big. I needed more time."

"You get what I give you tonight, sweetheart." He had to work to keep his tone even because she was squeezing him, making him want to forget about everything except fucking her hard. She felt so good. What he hadn't told her was that he'd never not used a condom. Not once in his fucking life. Never. And yet he'd wanted to know what it felt like with her. He'd wanted to know there wasn't anything in between them. Good. It felt so damn good. Warm and wet and safe. It was stupid but that word ran through his brain. She felt right.

But he had a job to do and he intended to get it done properly. He smacked her ass and she wiggled. It was going to be a test of his will not to come inside her before he finished. "Do you leave our damn bed without saying good-bye?"

He smacked her again, right on the gorgeous, fleshiest part of her ass.

She gasped and he could feel it on his freaking dick. "Nope. Although, again, I'm not sure how this is punishment. It feels so good. I don't think a spanking is supposed to feel this good."

He slapped her other cheek, three times in rapid succession. "Tell me how it feels."

He wanted to hear it from her. He started a rhythmic succession of spanks. One after another, each one causing her to wriggle and writhe on his dick, bringing them both pleasure.

"It hurts at first, but I even like that part. I like the fire on my skin. It wakes me up and makes me feel alive. Oh, I'm going to come," she breathed the words out.

He couldn't let that happen. He reached up and twisted a nipple, a tiny wrench to bring her back. "No, you're not. You will not like what happens if you come, Bridget. And don't think I can't tell. You are one of those blessed females who can't hide it or pretend because when you really come it gets messy."

She'd left a gorgeous wet spot where she'd come that first time. He loved the fact that she didn't hold back, couldn't fool him. When Bridget Slaten came, she screamed and dug her nails in and left evidence of her pleasure.

"That is the most embarrassing thing I've ever heard." She'd gone from a nice pink to a deep scarlet.

He got back to spanking her. He slapped at her skin and then held the heat there. "It's not embarrassing. Good sex is dirty and messy, and the night we spent together was the best fucking sex of my life."

"Seriously?" Her eyes found his as though looking for the truth.

He could show her the truth. He lifted her off his cock, almost all the way before slamming her back down. "You fuck me, Bridget. Ride my cock hard and make me forget what it felt like to wake up without you."

He wanted to forget everything but the way she felt when she clamped her pussy around him.

Bridget seemed to come alive. She'd held on to him before, but her eyes found his and her hands balanced on his shoulders as she started to ride him. Her hips found a rhythm that got those gorgeous tits bouncing.

"That was only fifteen. You promised me thirty. You promised."

"You fucking gorgeous brat." If she wanted everything he had, he would give it to her.

It was a race. Will smacked her ass as she rode his dick like a jockey on a racehorse. She groaned and slid up and down, her body moving in a sensual rhythm.

He didn't get this from one-night hookups with club subs. They'd all done what he asked, allowing him to bring them to pleasure and find his own, but Bridget challenged him. Bridget was going to make him earn her submission, and he wasn't sure he ever wanted her to simply lie back in bed. He loved the fight of sex with her, loved the fucking heat, loved the fact that he wasn't sure he was going to win.

Five more. Only five more.

She rotated her hips and he nearly went over the edge.

Three more.

She leaned back and he realized she was watching his cock slide in and out.

Fuck, he was going to die. As fast as he could, he laid the last three and then took control. "There. You got your thirty. Now I want mine. You come for me. You come all over my cock. You don't hold back a fucking thing."

He lifted her up and slammed her back down, and that was all it took. Her head fell back and she moaned as he felt her pussy clamp down around him.

The hot clasp of her cunt was enough to send him into overdrive. His whole body tightened as he came, pouring himself inside her. He fucked into her over and over until he was spent, having given her every ounce of come he had.

She fell on top of him, her head finding his neck. She was a limp doll draped around his body. "If that was punishment, Sir, I think I might be a bad girl."

He wrapped his arms around her. He suddenly had a thing for bad girls.

Chapter Seven

Bridget looked up as the door opened. It was weird. She hadn't quite gotten used to Will walking in on his own, but it seemed silly to not give the man a key when he showed up all hours of the day or night. His schedule sucked. During the time they'd been together, he'd gotten called into work twice in the middle of the night. Every other night, he'd spent in her bed or he'd taken her to his. If he wasn't working, he was with her and she'd found a comfort in it. They talked, really talked, and she found herself opening up to him. He'd finally asked her about the scar on her belly and she'd told him the story. He'd kissed it and then promptly gotten on the phone trying to track down her surgical records to make sure the doctor hadn't screwed up. Everything was perfect—except she was waiting for it to fall apart.

"Hey, I didn't expect you for a couple of hours."

He strode in and it was obvious he'd already stopped by his place. He was without his ever-present briefcase. Instead, he was carrying a bottle of champagne and two glasses. When he grinned at her, she was pretty sure her heart was going to explode. "I finished up early. Skaterboy is on the road to recovery and I am off work for two whole weeks. Do you have any idea how long it's been since I took two weeks off?"

The way he worked, maybe never. She gave him a smile, but she kind of wished he'd waited another hour or so to come by. The day had left her restless and she hadn't worked herself up to company mode. She'd been writing a sad passage of the book and then there was the fact that she knew their time together was coming to an end. She forced herself to try. "It sounds like you're looking forward to it."

His smile was steady. "You have no idea. We spend one in Hawaii and then…hell, why don't we spend two weeks in Hawaii? I've never been. I've heard it's beautiful and I want to spend the next fourteen days lying on a beach, drinking alcohol and fucking you. What do you say?"

"Our contract ends before then." It had been bugging her. Another thing that had her on edge. They had an end date. She'd read through that contract three times, telling herself she was doing it for research, but her heart always clenched when she saw the date written in.

"It doesn't have to." He set the bottle on the counter. "It's just a contract. We can amend it. I think we're working quite nicely."

Too nicely. They'd settled into a happy routine that she was worried she already needed to be content. He'd figured out how disorganized she was and spent four hours redoing her desk and making sure all her notes and series bibles were easy to find on her computer. They spent the evenings watching some movie or the news while he rubbed her feet or her scalp as she lay with her head in his lap. He didn't seem to be able to sit without having a hand on her, and she'd gotten used to being petted for hours every night.

How could she go back to being alone?

She knew she should let it be, knew she should do what she'd been planning on in the beginning and live in the moment. Unfortunately, she couldn't stop thinking about the future and when he was going to leave her. "So we amend the contract once a week?"

He popped the cork with an expert hand, but then he did everything with exquisite control. He poured her a half a glass. "I think that would be obnoxious. Let's go for a month this time. Here you go. Are you packed?"

He seemed so settled, so satisfied, when she was restless. She forced her irritation down. It wasn't his fault. She was worried about seeing her parents. It had been over two years since she'd had to do it. She'd only seen them then because her grandmother had died. Her father had made sure to let her know what he thought of her books. He'd found her pen name and without reading a single word, decided she was a purveyor of porn and wouldn't her grandmother be ashamed. She'd pointed out that Nana had been her first and best beta reader and that set off an awful fight.

Thinking about being in the same room with her self-righteous prick of a father unsettled her, and Will was acting like it was going to be a fun vacation.

"They won't like you. They don't like anyone. I think we should talk about how to handle them. Maybe we should go over some worst-case scenarios."

His lips curled up. "Maybe you should let me handle them. I'll take care of you, sweetheart."

She felt her fists clench at her sides and tried to force herself to relax. "You don't understand how nasty they can be."

And once he did, would he lump her in with the rest of them? She got even bitchier when she got around her family. He thought he'd seen Bratty Bridget? What would he think of Bitchy Bridget?

He stood in front of her, staring down with a calm affection that should have made her feel better. "I've dealt with meth dealers coming after my mother for money. I think I can handle one rich asshole. So calm down and say yes to staying with me and taking some real time off."

She shook her head. It seemed awfully dangerous to spend more time falling in love with the man. "I have a deadline."

"You have a deadline that's months off. You're ahead of schedule. I've already talked to your agent. She agrees with me. She loves me by the way. I told you, parents love a doctor."

"You called Maureen?" He was right about her agent. She kind of had been a mom to her for the last year. Since her first agent had died, Maureen had tried to take care of her, even bugging her to date again. She bet Maureen adored Will.

"She called and you were in the shower. I answered. We had a very nice chat about the fact that you need to take more time for yourself. You also need a PA. I talked to Chris about sharing one with you. Between the two of you, you could keep an assistant working full time. Maureen sent a list of qualified applicants. She's going to interview them while we're all in Hawaii."

"That was presumptuous." He was invading every part of her life, making her dependent on him when he was going to walk away at some point. He was like the rest of them, except worse because she needed him.

He stopped and set his glass down. "You know you need help."

"Then I'll find it myself." She had to be independent.

He stepped up and sighed, putting his hands on her face. "All right, I'll back off. I thought I was helping. Part of the whole Dom sub thing is that the Dom often decides he knows what's right and acts on it, thinking the sub will look at him like he's some kind of hero for butting in where he shouldn't."

Damn it. She did need one. She'd been putting it off because she had so much to do. If he were really her boyfriend, she would likely think nothing of it, but he wasn't staying around forever. Hell, after he met her family, he wouldn't want to stay the extra time.

"What's got that look on your face? Is it your family?" He leaned over and kissed her.

He was so fucking perfect, and she was waiting for it all to fall apart because she couldn't trust it. "I don't think I can stay the extra week."

He stepped back. "Why?"

He'd dropped the grin and now he stared at her in that same academic fashion he'd used before they'd signed their contract. She could feel him pulling away from her.

Maybe it was for the best. She could stay quiet and enjoy her last few days with him and then get out of the relationship with her dignity intact. She would move, naturally, because she couldn't watch him come and go every day and not be able to touch him, but he didn't have to know he'd broken her heart. She would also leave Sanctum and absolutely never return. She didn't have to write BDSM books. She would stick to ménage and vanilla romance. The point was, he didn't have to know what an idiot she was. She was going to tell him it was all about work and leave it at that.

Somehow her mouth and head weren't in synch on this one. "It all feels settled, Will, and I know it's not. You can amend the contract for a month and it buys me some time. I know you're comfortable living in the moment, but I'm not built for it. I need to know where I stand."

He leaned against the counter casually. "I told you where you stand. I want more time with you."

"A month." She knew she should stop, but something was pushing her. His actions told her one thing. That stupid contract said another, and she couldn't quite reconcile the two.

"We can start with a month and see where it goes from there. I don't understand why this bothers you. We're just having fun."

Did he not get it? She was on the verge of tears and she wasn't doing that in front of him. No way. "That's why it bothers me, Will. Exactly that. It doesn't feel like fun. It feels serious to me. You spend every night with me. We sleep together. We eat together. We play together. For god's sake, I've been wearing a butt plug for days so you can screw my ass. I don't know how much more intimate we can get but you still say we're just having fun."

"What more do you want from me?" His voice went hard, frustration evident. "I'm willing to sign a contract. I'm willing to spend time with you. I'm faithful to you. What the hell else do you want?"

"I want to know we're going to be together past the next month, damn it."

"I can sign a contract with you and then leave you tomorrow. You understand that, right? We could get married and I could divorce you. Nothing holds me to you, Bridget. Even that contract is only a piece of paper, but I'm willing to sign it and honor it. It won't hold me if I want to leave."

"But love would." She wanted to call the words back even as she said them. She was so stupid.

He groaned. "Do not throw that ridiculous word in my face. God, I thought you were more mature than that."

She could feel her skin flushing with embarrassment, but what had he expected? "I write romance novels, Will. My whole fucking life is about trying to find love."

He rolled his eyes and when he stepped away, he ran a frustrated hand through his hair. "And I was very explicit about what I wanted."

She was going to lose this fight. She'd known it in the back of her head, but her stomach dropped anyway. "Yes, you wanted a couple of weeks of sex."

"Don't you make me into the bad guy. I haven't fucked you and walked away. I've been here with you every night I could be. I haven't treated you with anything but respect and affection and I'm not the one trying to blow everything up over one freaking word."

"But I love you."

She watched as he took a deep breath and his shoulders settled. He seemed calmer when he turned.

"I'm glad, Bridget. I care about you. I don't believe in that particular word. I think it's something made up for greeting cards and to sell flowers, but if you believe in it then I'm glad you love me." He walked over to her and caught her hands in his. "Baby, don't do this over a word. What you call love, I call good teamwork. Compatibility. I am willing to admit to you that I started this relationship because I wanted to get into your bed so bad I could taste it, but I enjoy what we have. Do you have to have a declaration of love and eternal devotion to continue to spend time with me?"

So logical. He was calm and logical and it was sort of working on her. She was able to breathe. His hands were warm around hers, the steady strength of his body a real comfort to her. She was getting emotional and he was trying to ground her. Maybe he was right. Maybe they were speaking two different languages but it came to the same place.

Maybe she was being a crazy bitch because they'd only been dating for a week and she was asking for a lifetime. She looked up at him. He really was a spectacular man. "I'm sorry. I'm writing a scene that gets me emotional."

He sighed and leaned over to kiss her forehead. "I wish you would write a scene that got you horny." He pulled her close and when he touched her, she knew it was right. "It's going to be okay, baby. We're going to have fun. You'll see. I'll handle your parents. All I want you to think about is relaxing. No work. Okay?"

He was an optimist. She would give him that. "I will try."

His cell trilled and he groaned. "Damn it. It's the hospital. I told them to call if they had questions about the meds I prescribed. Give me a minute? I promise no calls after tonight. Just you and me."

And her wretchedly nasty family. But she gave him a nod and he answered the phone, striding back to the bedroom where he tended to take his work calls. She'd been nosy the first couple of times. She'd stood outside the door and listened in, some tiny part of her waiting to hear him talking to another woman. Unless words like ventriculostomy and craniectomy got women hot, he was all about the work.

There was a knock on her door. Pizza. They'd agreed that the night before a trip should definitely be pizza night, but again she'd expected it a little later.

She sighed. She was sure Kai would tell her that her anxiety stemmed from childhood issues of abandonment and the fact that the two men she'd previously had somewhat serious relationships with had turned out to be cheating douchebags, but she had to get over it. She had to find a way to trust him. If they had any shot at working this thing out, she had to put her issues aside and see Will for the man he was, not the men she'd dated before.

She opened the door and frowned. A woman stood there and she definitely wasn't carrying a large pepperoni with mushrooms. She looked like she never ate cheese in her life. Thin and lovely, she had perfectly straight platinum hair and wore a pair of heels that made her at least six inches taller than Bridget. "Can I help you?"

She bit into her bee-stung bottom lip and pointed to the door across the hall. "I know this seems stupid and I'm so sorry to bother you, but I was hoping you would know when Will Daley might get home. He's a doctor and he works certain shifts. Maybe you've seen him coming and going?"

Her gut knotted. This was definitely not one of Will's sisters. "Why?"

"I'm his girlfriend. His submissive, though you might not understand the term. I need him. If you have any way to contact him, please help me."

No. There was no way this was possibly happening to her. The woman in front of her was beyond gorgeous. Was she the woman who had hurt Will so badly he'd gone into his shell? Was she the reason he wouldn't use the word love? Because he'd loved her and he wouldn't love anyone else?

She felt stuck. Trapped. Like suddenly her feet were glued to the ground and she couldn't pull away. "His sub? He's your Master?"

"Yes." She sighed as though relieved. "You understand. Good. Then you know that he would want to help me. I'm in trouble. I'm likely to endure a very long spanking, but I've realized how good I had it with him. He's a kind man and he loves me. I need to speak with him as soon as possible."

"He told you he loves you?" An ache began somewhere deep inside.

"Many times, but I was too foolish to return it until now. Do you know what kind of shift he's working this week? His hours can be odd, but he's usually home at night. He tried to work his schedule so I wouldn't be alone, so he could protect me."

He'd probably treated her like a princess. He'd probably never poked her awake and asked her to drive him to the hospital at two in the morning because he needed to look over some notes before an emergency procedure. No, this blonde goddess would be "protected."

"Bridget? Is the pizza here? I'm starving."

She turned and he was stopped in the middle of her living room, his eyes on the woman in the doorway.

"Starr?"

Starr smiled brilliantly and nearly trampled Bridget in her haste to get to her Master. She threw herself against him. "Master, I've missed you so much."

His hands went to her arms, peeling her off his body. "This is a conversation we should have in private." He pulled his keys out of his pocket. "Go to my place. You seem to know where it is. We'll have a conversation about that, too."

He was all Dom now. No hint of her teasing lover.

Starr sniffled and turned. A single teardrop clung to her cheek. Bitch even cried pretty. When Bridget cried, she became an ugly, sobbing mess. Like Jabba the Hutt except with snot. Which was precisely why she wasn't going to cry.

"Yes, Master. I'll wait for you. I've missed you so much. I've been such a fool." She gave Bridget a nasty stare as she exited stage left.

A heavy silence hung over them.

Will finally moved, his eyes on the door. "I'll be back in a few minutes."

Bridget stepped in his path. "Who was that?"

She knew the story, but apparently not the whole of it, and she'd never heard it from his side. He never talked about his past except in snarky witticisms. When she tried to scratch the surface, he always changed the subject or kissed her until she couldn't breathe.

"It's not any of your business, Bridget. I'll handle it."

She shook her head. "She said she's your sub. I think that makes it my business."

His lips quirked up in a big jerk smile. "She lies. Now step aside. I won't be more than ten minutes."

"You won't be anything at all if you don't talk to me." She was screwing this up. "I'm sorry. I need to know."

"Are you giving me an ultimatum?" He wasn't looking at her. He was staring at the hallway, likely at his door, as though his whole being was already in that room with her, with Starr.

"I need to know. Please talk to me." She could deal with it if he was honest with her.

"You don't need to know. I've told you everything you need to know. I wrote it all out in that contract. If you're worried I'm going over there to fuck her, you can rest assured I wouldn't touch that woman with a ten-foot pole. I will handle the situation and come back to you and we'll eat dinner and get ready for our flight tomorrow."

"You have got to be kidding me." He couldn't expect her to ignore what had happened.

"Bridget, move out of my way and do it now. I'm talking to you as your Dominant partner. Either stand down and let me deal with this or break our contract right here and now."

She stepped back, allowing him access to the exit. Her heart was thudding in her chest, but she was pleased with the even tone of her voice. "Now who's giving out ultimatums?"

He turned at the door. "Bridget…"

Now he wanted to talk? Oh, he'd made himself perfectly clear. She held up a hand. "No, please. Don't let me keep you."

She slammed the door in his face as the tears began to fall. There was a hard thud against the door like he'd smacked it in frustration, but then she listened and heard him take the necessary steps, heard his door open and close.

Before it could escape, Bridget shoved her hand over her mouth, stopping the sob that wouldn't stay inside. Tears blurred her world as the truth hit her. She was in love with a man who couldn't even be bothered to explain why another woman had shown up at her door.

He really did view her as a good time. He might stay around. He might honor that month-long contract he talked about, but he would never love her. He would never want forever.

She locked the door and then turned the dead bolt it so he couldn't use a key to get back in. He'd made himself plain. She was good for sex and fun and she had no place in his real life. A woman like Starr had. When the good doctor settled down—and she had no doubt that he would eventually—it would be with someone gorgeous and deeply submissive. It wouldn't be with a girl who everyone knew was a brat.

When the pizza came, she slid two twenties to the delivery boy and asked him to give the pizza to the first homeless man he came to and then locked the door again.

Oddly, she'd lost her appetite.

* * * *

Will closed the door behind him and wondered how he was going to get back into Bridget's place. His brat had undoubtedly dead bolted the door, and she would likely do anything to keep him out.

He couldn't let that happen. He also couldn't let her know about Starr. God, what the hell would she think if she knew what an idiot he'd been? The object of his idiocy sat on his sofa with her legs crossed, looking every inch the lady when he knew damn well she was so much more. Liar. User. Accessory to murder.

"I don't want you here. Please leave and don't return."

"You quit your job in Fort Worth," she said, her voice quiet. She always talked in that soft voice. At first he'd found it haunting and peaceful that she never raised her tone. Now he found it annoying. How the hell was he supposed to know what she was feeling? Bridget always let him know. Usually with force.

But she should trust him enough to deal with this. What the fuck was that ultimatum? She wanted to give him ultimatums? He didn't deal well with them.

Of course, he'd then thrown one in her face, and he kind of got the feeling she didn't deal well with them either. Damn it.

"Master?"

She was still here. He hoped if he ignored her she would disappear, but the world wasn't that kind.

"Don't call me that. How did you find me?"

"There was a nurse at the hospital who told me you're working in Dallas now. I had a friend look you up. You were on the white pages on the Internet. I didn't do anything illegal, Mast…Will." Tears clung to her eyes, perfectly placed and perfectly fucking fake like the rest of her.

He bet if Bridget cried she would get red and blotchy and he would have to soothe her. He would have to hold her to calm her down, but only after he'd protected his balls because his Bridget got angry first.

When had he started thinking of her as his? When had he started spending large parts of his day plotting how to get her in the right mood, how to make her happy or to calm her down when someone cut them off on the freeway or to soothe her when she read something crappy about her books?

He'd never had to do that with Starr. Nope. She was always right there to please her Master. Never said a harsh word until he found she'd been lying to him the whole time. "Why are you here? The last time we talked I believe you called me a freak who abused you."

Thank god for Karina talking him into going to Sanctum, and to Kai for listening to him, or he likely would have gone back into the closest, so to speak.

She turned her gorgeous face up to him. He could see the perfection there but suddenly she was so much less appealing than Bridget's sweet face—even though she was probably mad as shit with him, but she was wrong about that. This was his problem. It was his right to keep her the hell out of it. He didn't even like the fact that Starr knew Bridget existed. "I've had a lot of time to think, William."

"Yes, I've heard jail can do that for a girl," he drawled.

She sniffled and nodded. "You're right. You're always right." This was the point when Bridget would shove her middle finger his way and tell him to fuck off and then he would playfully chase her down and spank her. Starr merely stood and lowered herself into a submissive pose. "I've had time to really understand what you want from me and what I need. I was scared. I was scared of how much I felt for you. Of how much I loved our life together."

"I was scared of how close I came to getting syphilis. How many other dudes were you doing?" Damn it. Bridget was rubbing off on him.

She shook her head. "There was only Terry. He forced me to be with him, and now I understand why. I am submissive and he abused my submission. He took it when he didn't earn it. I can see now that you saw my true nature and tried to rescue me."

"Are you fucking kidding me? Let me get this straight. He forced you to sleep with him. He forced you to sleep with me. He forced you to aid and abet in the murders of four women. And he forced you to do everything you could to pin it all on me, including pumping heroin through my veins and stuffing me in the back of my car. My knee still aches from that. Thanks a lot."

She wouldn't meet his eyes, preferring to keep her head down. "Yes. That's what I'm saying. He used my submissive nature to force me to do his will."

"Are you going to use that in court? My submission made me do it? Let me tell you something. That's the biggest load of crap I've ever heard and it goes to prove that you've learned absolutely nothing. A submissive is strong. She's as strong as her Dom." Like Bridget was strong. "You made the choices you made and you'll pay the price. You had every opportunity to tell me what was going on. I would have helped you. I would have made sure that dickhead boyfriend of yours stopped before he killed four women. Four. That's on you and that will not go away, and it cannot be explained by crying and saying you're not responsible. I do not love you. I will not help you. I will, in fact, be getting a restraining order against you."

Her head came up and he saw the minute she dropped the act. "Please. I can't go back to jail. I can't. It's horrible there. I'll do whatever you want. I'll be the little doll you seem to need. I did it before and I'll do it again. Please testify in my favor. You can do anything you want to me, Will."

His stomach rolled. "Get out of my house. I really am getting that restraining order. If you want to have any hope in a court of law, you better not show your face again."

She stood and her mouth became a flat, angry line. "I should have known you wouldn't help me. You fucking freak. You make me sick."

He opened the door for her. "The feeling is mutual."

She strode past him, angry tears in her eyes.

And he was left staring at the door across the hall. He didn't owe Bridget an explanation. He'd handled the problem and while they were in Hawaii, Mitch would get the restraining order in place.

He thought briefly about moving, but abandoned the idea. He liked being close to Bridget.

He needed to be close to her. Fuck.

He crossed the space between their places and knocked on the door. Nothing.

He tried his key. Yep. She'd used the deadbolt.

Fuck and double fuck. If he tried to talk to her tonight, she would likely tell him they were through. He had to figure out what her next move would be.

Probably leaving for the flight without him. He wasn't sure of which flight it was or which private airport. Bridget had handled all of those details. He only knew when the car was coming to pick them up.

But someone else knew.

Sneaky. He had to be sneaky if he wanted to get her back without having to tell her what an idiot he'd been.

The good news was, he'd perfected the art of battle when it came to Bridget Slaten.

He had to pray he could win the war.

Chapter Eight

It had been too easy. The door to the sedan opened and she slipped out of the car that had come to pick her up. It was late, the sky dark all around her.

God, she missed Will. It had only been a few hours and she felt the loss.

She'd heard him knock the night before and had thought about opening the door to see if he would actually talk to her about what had happened. She'd decided to leave it be. He'd been plain with her. He didn't love her. Never would. The most she would get out of him was a few more weeks.

Should she have taken them? She looked at the private jet. It had been years since she'd been on one. She was kind of proud of the fact that she could afford first class now on her own, but she definitely couldn't have this.

She'd wanted to share this with Will. She'd really wanted that last couple of days with him.

"Ms. Slaten, would you care to board? We leave in five minutes. The other guest is already in place," the driver said, gesturing toward the stairs that would lead her to the plane.

She nodded and started up them, her mind on Will. What was he doing? He'd obviously decided to let her leave without him. Maybe he was with Starr. Maybe he'd knocked on her door to tell her that he was happy he had his serial-killer-helping ex-submissive back. Maybe he was far too busy screwing her right now to even think about the fact that he'd seriously fucked Bridget over.

Guest? She looked back at the driver to ask him about the other guests. There was supposed to be seven other guests. Serena and her husbands, Chris and his Dom, and Ian and Charlotte Taggart were supposed to be on that plane. The McKay-Taggart crew was coming out to talk to her father and ensure security for the wedding. It was precisely why her dad had sent the big jet.

Shit. She looked at the freaking plane. It was the smaller of the two her dad used. Damn it. There had been a mistake. She and her sister called this one the love jet because it was the one their dad used when he escorted his mistresses around. It came complete with a bedroom.

She groaned as she walked up the stairs because the driver had taken off. She would have to get answers from the pilot or the attendant. They couldn't fit everyone in this stupid plane.

And she still hadn't figured out what she was going to tell her sister. The day was turning into one massive cluster fuck and she wasn't even looking forward to yelling at someone.

Her cell trilled, signaling a text was coming through, and she pulled it out of her bag as she entered the plane.

Shit. Speak of the devil. Her sister. Damn, but she hated the fact that she'd let Amy down. She touched the screen to read the message.

Can't wait 'til you get here. Frankie is fabulous. You'll love him like I do. And we both love your guy. So sweet. Have a great flight and give Will a big kiss for me. I know this is a fake engagement, but after talking to him, I think it should become the real thing. That man is a keeper. See you soon.

Bridget frowned. When the hell had Amy talked to Will?

She stepped on the plane, ready for some answers.

"Hello? Does anyone realize this is the wrong plane? Where are we going to put the seven of us and the baby? He can't go in the damn cargo hold."

A polished and perfectly made up flight attendant greeted her with a glass of wine in hand. She had to give it to her father; the man did know how to fly. Oh, he'd gotten there on the backs of the little people, but he wasn't chintzy with the good wine. "Ms. Slaten, it's a pleasure to have you with us today. Your sister is a favorite of ours. She's asked us to take excellent care of you and we're happy to do so. Dinner will be served once we reach our cruising altitude and you'll find I've already turned down the bed. Our flight time is seven hours and fifty minutes. I'll make sure you're awake an hour before we land. If you need anything, don't hesitate to ask."

"Yeah, I need to know where everyone else is." She took the wine though. She would need it to get through the whole shebang. Maybe if she stayed drunk for the next week, it would fly by.

The flight attendant shook her head. "The other party went out on the larger jet about an hour ago. Your sister changed the plans last night. This is her gift to you. Privacy. Enjoy."

She shook her head as she made her way into the luxurious lounge. To the back of the plane would be the kitchen, bar, study, and bedroom complete with thousand thread count sheets.

Yeah. Why had Amy thought she would need privacy? Well, at least she knew now when Amy had talked to Will.

"How did you know her phone number, Daley?" She wasn't a complete idiot.

He stepped out of the hall that led to the bar. He looked utterly delicious in slacks and an open-necked white dress shirt. "I called Serena last night and told her I wanted to set up a surprise for you. She was willing to help. Do you like the wine? I made sure they had the Sauvignon Blanc you love."

She took a drink because it was not the grapes' fault and they shouldn't go to waste. "You should leave now."

She heard the thud as the airplane door was closed and sealed. Well, that was her fault for almost being late. He'd used that to his advantage, too.

He stared at her with big, gorgeous dark eyes. Stupid eyes that made her want to melt at his surprisingly attractive feet. She normally didn't like feet, but his were the exception. "I understand you're angry, but you don't have any reason to be. That woman means nothing to me."

She'd meant enough to him to blow up their evening. "She did once."

"And she doesn't now. She has no effect on us whatsoever. I

understand why you locked the door."

That surprised her. Now that she thought about it, he was very tolerant of her emotional reactions. "What? You're not going to accuse me of being childish?"

"No, I'm not. You often overreact to situations, but once you calm down, you see reason. I've gotten used to it. You're a passionate woman. It's one of the things I like about you. You needed to show me how you felt. Well, I understand. I can promise you that it won't happen again. I've taken steps to make sure she never bothers us again."

"I would like to know why she was bothering us in the first place."

His jaw tightened. "She's a former submissive of mine. It didn't work out, but I make it a habit to not talk about my relationships. I would give you the same courtesy."

Anger welled. He thought he'd seen her overreact? "So you're lumping me in with the girl who tried to pin a couple of murders on you?"

His face went white. "How do you know about that?"

He thought she didn't know? "We talk in the club. Everyone knows, Will. Every single person in that club knows that you fell in love with a perfect sub and she turned out to be a crazy bitch who was using you for the man she really loved. It's a juicy story. You couldn't expect that no one would tell it."

His face went blank, but not before she'd seen the startled hurt in his eyes.

Damn her mouth. She never knew when to shut up. But wasn't she in the right? He was the one who told her it was none of her business.

He nodded. "I'll see if I can stop the plane."

He moved past her and she rushed into the study to get away from him. She couldn't freaking breathe. He hadn't argued with her. Hadn't violently protested that her account was wrong. Maybe she was right and he did love that crazy woman.

It was good to have it out. She wasn't anyone's rebound girl. She strode into the bedroom because she wasn't going to watch him leave now that she'd called him out.

She stopped. The bed was covered in rose petals. White ones. Her favorites. And there was a tray of chocolate-covered strawberries. Also her favorites. He'd gone to a lot of trouble for the rebound girl.

She'd been mean. Maybe he'd been mean, too, but now that she thought about it, a story like that getting around would hurt Will's pride.

And to hear it coming from the woman he'd been sleeping with? Yeah, that had to hurt.

Was she going to let him walk away like that? At the very least, she should apologize.

She turned, but he was standing in the doorway, blocking her way. "I need to get my kit and I'll go. I can call a cab at the office."

All of her anger fled and she was left with a sadness that threatened to bring her low. "I'm sorry."

He held a hand up. "Hey, it's no problem. I thought I could keep it quiet. You're right. It's a juicy story."

Deflecting. He was good at that. He was also damn good at calming her down, but he was the one who needed soothing. Was he embarrassed? Was that the reason he'd cut her out and tried to hide the meeting? "Please don't go. You don't have to go to the wedding with me, but could we talk for a minute?"

"I don't think there's anything left to say."

She'd thought about nothing but herself and her own issues since the horrible night before began. She hadn't once thought about what he needed. He'd been honest with her, even when it hurt his cause. "I think there is. I'm sorry. I was so mad at you for leaving with her. No. I'm lying. It wasn't anger, Will. It was blinding jealousy. I was so jealous."

He didn't move, but she saw the moment his eyes softened. "You had nothing to be jealous of."

"She's beautiful, Will."

"Maybe on the outside, but I'll be honest, she was always too thin for my tastes. If you're looking for someone to tell you you're beautiful, I believe I've done that about a thousand times. Now, I'd like to get out of here with some dignity. The plane needs to take off."

She wouldn't see him again if she let him get off the plane. He was right. She did overreact and then she put herself in a corner she couldn't get out of. Was she going to let that one incident sour everything else? She'd spent the best week of her life with him and then she'd turned on him the minute he did something she didn't like.

"Please don't leave. I'm sorry I said what I said."

"You told me the truth."

"No. I said something meant to hurt you. Will, I've known about what happened since before we started dating. I didn't think less of you when I heard that story."

"Sure." He was obviously tense, every line of his body rigid. He seemed to be simply trying to survive until she let him go.

He'd gotten so good at soothing her. How could she not know how to do the same for him? Affection. He responded to affection and he struggled to reject it.

She stepped up and before he could move away from her, she wrapped her arms around his waist. "I don't think less of you, Will. God, that would be the most hypocritical thing I could do. Did you listen to my dating life? I've gotten used by every man I've dated up to you. Does that make me a fool? An idiot?"

"No, sweetheart." His voice had softened. "It makes you a little naïve and that's not a bad thing. But we're talking about two completely different things here."

"Nope. They're the same. Why is this a problem? Are you mad that I asked about you?"

He stayed still and after a moment, she felt his hands on her hair. "Gossiping is a spankable offense. It's in our contract." He breathed again, his hands tightening. "You really don't think less of me?"

She turned her face up. "Are you freaking kidding me? Will, think about it for two seconds. Would I have signed that contract if I thought you were some sort of pathetic loser? I knew what had happened to you before I ever agreed to sub for you. I was being a bitch because I was hurt that you chose her over me."

His fingers tangled in her hair and he forced her to look into his eyes. "I did no such thing. I chose to handle a situation without drawing you into my problems. I didn't know that you were a nosy brat so I was trying to keep my sad past from you."

She still had so many questions. "What did you see in her?"

He sighed, but she felt a shift. He wasn't so anxious. He'd relaxed slightly. "I don't think that's important, but let's get the plane in the air and we'll talk about it. Can we agree to spend this last week together?"

"Two weeks." She wanted all the time she could get with him. If he had two weeks of vacation, she wanted it. Anyhow, anyway she could get it.

"Tell me why."

There was only one reason. She was so tired of lying. He knew her. He seemed to see right through her, and there was comfort in that. "Because I love you."

"And I don't believe in the word."

Maybe her love was the important thing here. Maybe it was more important to love than to have it returned. It would be perfect if he could love her back, but this feeling she had made her better. Loving him made her better. "So we agree to disagree. It's okay. Do you want to be with me?"

"So much it hurts, sweetheart."

That was all she could ask. It would end. It was inevitable. He would say he didn't believe in love right up until the moment he found the woman who made him. But she was pretty sure he was the love of her life. She would take these weeks and hold them close to her heart, and she would let him go at the end so he could find the woman who would set him free.

Damn it, growing up hurt like hell. "Then let's go to a wedding. Let's have our vacation."

He smiled, the sight pleasing her more than she could imagine. "Let's do it."

* * * *

Will polished off the last of the very excellent steak the attendant had served them. The rich really were different. Apparently they employed gourmet chefs who made perfectly cooked steaks at thirty thousand feet and knew how a martini should be shaken.

He set down his glass. If he had much more he wouldn't be able to play with her, and that was definitely going to happen. He needed it. He needed to be back in control even if it was only in the bedroom.

He'd managed to talk about innocuous things throughout dinner. They'd talked about her sister and how Bridget and Amy had grown up. Private schools and nannies. There had been one in particular Bridget talked about. Nanny Christine. She'd been with her from third grade through Amy's graduation. From what Will could tell, she'd been more of a mother to the two girls than their biological mom.

Bridget sat back. "That was so good. Did you tell them what to cook?"

He knew what she liked. He'd explained everything he wanted to Amy the night before. He wanted perfection. He wanted her smiling. Damn it. He wanted her to forgive him. "You like steak. You also like potatoes. And you like chocolate and strawberries. They're in the bedroom, though."

"Then we should probably head that way." She took another long sip of the wine he'd specifically ordered for her.

She was so fucking pretty with her raven black hair lazing past her shoulders and pointing the way right to those breasts he wanted to put his mouth on. She didn't think he was an idiot for what had happened. She wasn't shirking away from his trouble. Though maybe she didn't understand that it wasn't over.

"You know I'll have to go to court to testify, right?" It would be a huge pain in his ass. And the trial would likely be covered in the press.

Bridget's eyes went wide. "Do you have to meet with a lawyer?"

Shit. She was worried. "Mitch is my lawyer, but we'll have to go meet with the DA."

"Can I ask questions? Do you know the DA? Do you think he would let me shadow him for a week or so? I have this great idea about a DA and the witness to a murder. Well, and the defense attorney, but you will be shocked at how I work him into that threesome. Hint. The DA is bi."

Something relaxed inside him. Bridget wouldn't judge him. She was far too busy trying to figure out how his tragedy would aid in her research. "I don't think the DA will find time, but I assure you Mitch will. He owes me." He stood up, his body thrumming with anticipation. "Is our contract still valid?"

She nodded, but he couldn't miss the way her eyes dimmed. "Yes. I told you. I want to spend the next two weeks with you."

His gut did a weird flip at her words. Two weeks. A vacation. He'd been the one who posited the notion, but somehow he didn't like the idea of her thinking in terms of weeks. "I believe I offered you a contract for a month."

A long sigh came from her chest. "A month then."

He knew he should be satisfied that she was falling in line, but something about it unsettled him. He shoved the worry aside because he needed something from her. The plane was running smoothly. There were at a cruising altitude and it was time to spend a few hours resting before they had to meet her family.

He needed to concentrate on the positive. She knew the worst stuff about him—knew his mom was in and out of jail, currently serving a nice ten-year stint for trafficking because she was always trying to push the envelope on awfulness, knew he'd been a dumbass who thought he'd found the perfect sub when all he'd found was trouble. She knew all that and she was still sitting across from him. She'd still apologized for being a righteous bitch. He didn't blame her for that. She'd been upset and that was how Bridget communicated. He hadn't told her that he doubted he would have actually walked away. He'd been trying to find a way out from the moment she'd told him she knew.

He was incapable of walking away from her. God, he couldn't even keep his freaking hands off her.

"Come here." He wanted her close. It had been too long. Twenty-four freaking hours was too long to not have her sitting in his lap, to not be able to smell her all around him.

He'd always known he'd inherited an addictive personality from his meth-head mom. He'd taken pains to stay away from drugs, to limit himself to one or two beers or cocktails. But he couldn't limit himself with her. He had to have her. When he didn't have her, he was plotting and planning ways to get her. Like a fucking addict.

Was it wrong to be addicted to a person?

She stood up and in a second, she was lowering herself onto his lap, her arms going around his shoulders, and he didn't fucking care. If it was wrong then he didn't want to be right. He was cool with craving her. It felt good to give in for once in his life. He was all about discipline, but he could revel in her.

She turned her face up to his and he wanted to forget about everything except getting inside her, but she was owed some answers. He brushed his mouth against hers. It would be easier to talk when they were naked.

Without another thought, he shoved his arm under her knees, his other around her back, and stood up.

She gasped, clinging to his neck. "I really love it when you carry me. I don't want you to throw out your back though."

"Oh, you did not say you were heavy." He strode through the narrow confines of the hallway past the elegant study and into the bedroom. All in all, the plane was nicer than his condo. Bridget's dad was loaded.

She flushed nicely. "No. I merely stated that I hope your back health remains well."

He tossed her on the bed. "No. You don't get away so easily. Strip and put your ass in the air. I want it high, sweetheart."

She groaned but started to make quick work of her clothes. He shoved out of his too after closing the door behind them. It was definitely time to join the mile-high club, and he wanted to do it in spectacular fashion. He wanted to make sure she was so satisfied she forgot to worry about the upcoming wedding.

How bad could her parents really be?

He chucked his clothes and grabbed his kit. It was definitely nice to fly private. He didn't have to worry about freaking out the TSA with his assorted collection of torture devices. When he turned, he had to catch his breath.

She was on her knees, that juicy, glorious ass of hers in the air. Her breasts were pressed against the silky bedsheets. He'd felt like an idiot spreading rose petals all over the bed in an attempt to please her, but now he was happy he'd done it because they looked gorgeous against her skin. She was a submissive present all for him. Only for him.

"Do you know how beautiful you are?"

She turned her head, and the sensual smile on her face hit him squarely in the chest. "Why don't you tell me?"

He opened his kit. "I'll tell you. I'll tell you what you want to know. Bridget, I'm not much for talking about my past. I don't like to think about it much, but I'm going to make you understand that you're not some fill-in for her. You're more like a reward for surviving my own stupidity."

"If you call yourself stupid again, I get to spank you."

He couldn't help but smile back because she was a fierce thing when she wanted to be. And she had a point. Sometimes Doms needed a firm hand, too. Perhaps it was time to forgive himself for that idiocy. "Agreed. Baby, do you know what I'm going to do to you?"

She shivered, the motion going up and down her spine. "You're going to take my ass, aren't you?"

He put a hand on her perfectly formed cheeks. He adored how round and healthy they were and loved the twin dimples in the small of her back. "Yes, I am. I'm going to fuck this lovely asshole but not until we get it ready."

He gave her a hard smack and loved the way she gasped and moaned.

"Now, I'm going to explain a few things to you." Another spank. He held his hand to her flesh to keep the heat in. "I didn't have much of a sex life to speak of while I was in med school and during the first couple of years of my residency."

"So it's not like…"

"No. It's not like TV. Honestly, we're too tired to hump in the on-call rooms. I didn't have time for anything like a relationship." He kept up the slow spanking, punctuating his sentences with nice smacks that got her skin pink and pretty. "Now that I think about it, my relationships have been fairly casual. Even in high school and college, I had to work and watch after my sisters. I had a few girlfriends, but they tended to be a lot like me. Ambitious. Practical. We understood what was expected of each other. They weren't looking for anything past companionship, sex, and a regular date night."

"So no crazy, overly emotional creative types?"

That earned her a hard smack. "No. I would have told you I didn't want that, but I think we work well together." Yeah, that was romantic. "Anyway, after my residency was over, I started to look around for something more permanent, and that was when I found my first club. I went with a work colleague who understood my needs. It was an underground club. Not like Sanctum."

Her head started to come up. "Can…"

"No, I will not take you there for research." The sight of her ass was distracting him. His cock was throbbing pleasantly, patient since it knew it would get what it wanted. "It's dangerous, sweetheart. Those clubs are what got me in trouble in the first place."

"You met her there?" She gasped when he brought his hand down again.

"Yes. I met her and I was going through a slightly obsessive phase. I thought I wanted a truly submissive partner. Not just in the bedroom. Do you understand what I mean?" He spanked her harder this time. Her skin was warming up. It really was easier to talk about this when he had the distraction of her beauty to take away the humiliation he'd felt.

"Like you had to pick out her clothes and stuff?"

That had only been the beginning. "And leave a list of things for her to do and what she could eat. It was overwhelming, but I thought I should try. It seemed to be what she wanted. She was very peaceful. We moved fast because she gave me this story about how her ex-boyfriend was stalking her."

"I would have bought a gun."

He didn't doubt that at all. Bridget wouldn't have looked for a protector. She would have protected herself. "Of course you would. You would have turned it all around on him, but she wasn't anything like you, sweetheart. She also didn't actually have a stalker. She played me perfectly. I wanted to be the white knight, so I let her move in with me and we started a D/s relationship. You have to understand, I was very used to women being dependent on me. It felt almost natural."

"Because of your sisters."

"Yes, though they seem to be independent now. I rarely have to intercede on their behalves."

"Because you raised them right."

"I was a kid. I did what I could. I thought I could do the same for Starr. I thought she needed me. I now know you need me way more than she ever could."

"Hey, I'm the chick who would have bought the gun," Bridget admitted.

He didn't like to think about an armed Bridget. "And then likely murdered someone with it. No, baby. You have anger issues. And organizational issues. And you can't say no. You're overcommitted at work, and we're going to talk about that because you need relaxation time."

She also needed him. More than he'd imagined. When he'd gone into the relationship, he'd thought they would come together for play and sex, and then he'd realized she needed more than a casual Dom. She kind of needed a sneaky one. Unlike the other subs he'd played with, Bridget often rankled at the idea of an authority figure taking control over her life. So he'd quietly topped her. He wondered if she'd even noticed that he'd started handling things like her mail pile? Aside from that one night, he handled dinner since she ate crap. Had she noticed her fridge now boasted actual food? Probably not. Sneaky Dom. He kind of liked it.

"This isn't relaxing, Will. It's frustrating."

He could hear the little whine in her voice that let him know she was on the edge and really wanted to go over. He let his fingers glide over her labia, feeling the arousal there. She was wet. The spanking was already doing its job. He rubbed his thumb over her clit and felt the shiver go through her.

And then pulled his hand away because it wasn't going to be that easy. Not tonight. "It'll be relaxing in the end."

"Damn it."

He chuckled as he reached for the already prepped anal plug. "I promise I won't leave you unsatisfied. I want you to understand fully that

I'm not pining for Starr. I took out a restraining order on her. If you see her, I want you to call me. Don't ever open the door to her again."

He would be happier when she was safely in prison.

"So you weren't in love with her. Oh, my god. I can't get used to that." She reacted to the lube he squeezed on her asshole.

He liked the way it clenched and tried to keep him out. Like the rest of Bridget, her anus was a challenge. Yeah, he wasn't going to tell her that. She would likely shove an anal plug where he wouldn't want one. She would do it while he was sleeping. His sub was sneaky, too. He rimmed her with the tip, lubing the plug while he worked her asshole. "I told you. I've never been in this magical thing you call love. Do you want me to say it? I can if that's what you require."

"No. No. It's fine. It's better to be honest."

He wished he hadn't broached the subject at all. He needed to make it plain that he wasn't wishing for his lost love and trying to replace her. "I'm here with you, Bridget. I don't want to be anywhere else."

"For now."

Damn it. "I don't have any other time to give you."

Her ass wiggled. "Then you should really give me the now, if that includes making good on the promises you made. I believe there was something about being satisfied."

She moved with a sensuous grace, her hips rolling against the plug, but he couldn't help but feel some of the fire had gone out of her. Was this what Kai had warned him about? Did he not have what Bridget needed? Did she need the kind of man who could throw her his heart and say all the right things?

It didn't matter. He wasn't going to think about it. He was going to be a selfish bastard and he knew it. He was going to take every single thing she offered him and he wouldn't look back. His cock jumped at the sight of the plastic plug sinking inside her.

"This is a large plug, sweetheart. You took it beautifully. You're ready for me." He fucked her slowly with the plug, watching as her asshole opened and then tried to close. But he wasn't about to let that happen. No. He had her right where he wanted her.

"I don't know if I like it." Her hands were fisted around the sheets, her body taut.

He needed to relax her. Her ass might be ready but she was still thinking. He could practically hear her brain whirling. She never stopped unless he blotted out everything else for her.

"Hold tight to that plug. Concentrate and don't lose it."

"Why? What are you going to do?"

"This." He flipped her over as fast as he could so she was face up.

Her eyes narrowed as she seemed to take inventory. "Okay. I managed to keep the damn thing in. Will, I don't know that this is going to work. It's not like I haven't tried it before. I don't know that I like it. It feels like a whole lot of pressure."

She would keep talking until he made her stop. Bridget could talk for hours. But he'd found one sure way to stop the barrage of words that came out when she was anxious. He leaned over and started to suck on her clit.

"Oh. Oh. Oh."

Yes, that was so much better than her giving him all the reasons she wouldn't like anal. He knew damn well why she hadn't liked it before. Her previous lovers had been shitty. For a woman who wrote about sex, she hadn't had a lot of good fucking.

At least he could give her that.

Damn he was a selfish bastard, but he couldn't leave her. He couldn't. She shook as she came, and that was his cue to take what he wanted.

He spread her legs wide and pulled the plug free, stopping only long enough to lube up his cock. He was hard as a rock in anticipation of getting inside her again. He wanted to fuck her everywhere, any hole he could fit his dick in. Sex had always been an itch to scratch, but it was more with Bridget. Being with Bridget filled him in some unnamed way.

He pressed his cock to her asshole and started working his way in.

Bridget groaned. "You're a manipulative man, you know that, right? Now I can't tense up. I still don't think I'll like it."

Her body was languid under his, the orgasm doing exactly what he'd wanted it to do. She was relaxed and happy and willing to see where he would take her. She lay open to him. It was the only time she was truly submissive. And oddly, when he had her like this, he felt like he'd finally earned it.

He pressed his cockhead past the tight ring of muscles protecting her. Fuck. So tight. She was tight around him, and the heat was different than her pussy. It wasn't better, simply different. But he had to admit, he loved the way she started to squirm under him.

"You're too big." She bit her bottom lip, her eyes still lazy from her recent orgasm. "Oh, Will. I don't know. Oh, that feels…give me more."

He pressed in ruthlessly, his cock in a state of desperation. He fed his length deep inside as she spread her legs and moved her hips as though she couldn't wait for more. "You don't seem uncomfortable, sweetheart."

"You know I am and, oh, it feels different."

Because she'd been properly prepared and he'd trained her to expect pleasure from him. Because he never took and gave nothing back. "I want you to love this."

"I love you." Her hands found his backside, and he groaned as she sunk her nails in.

"I need you." It was the closest he could come, but it was also the truth. She was rapidly becoming necessary to him in a way he'd never imagined.

He dragged his cock back out almost to the end. Bridget gasped, her asshole clenching around him, trying to keep him inside now.

He let go because she was on the edge, too. He could see it in her breathing, the way her mouth had come open, how her hips moved in time with his. He fucked her ass hard, and she gave as good as she got. Over and over he worked his way in and then pulled out.

Bridget damn near screamed the plane out of the sky when she came. He adored the fact that she didn't know how to hold back. She let herself feel, let him know how she felt.

And she was happy, so that meant he could be happy, too. He gave over as his balls shot off. He stiffened above her, coming until he had nothing left to give her, pumping his semen deep inside.

He pulled out and rolled to the side, his body immediately nestling against hers.

"That did not suck, Daley."

He grinned and pulled her close. Nope. It definitely hadn't sucked.

Chapter Nine

Bridget waved to her sister as they entered the beautifully decorated private lanai overlooking the ocean. She hadn't seen her sister in months, but Amy looked lovely in a Chanel dress Bridget was fairly certain she couldn't fit her left butt cheek into and sky-high Louboutins. Still, she let it go since she'd gotten some sleep and Will seemed determined to prove that he could get it up and get it on at least once an hour. Her whole body felt pleasantly sore as she walked toward her sister.

All in all, she felt halfway decent for a woman stepping into the ninth ring of Hell. Will's hand tangled with hers and when she looked up at him, he gave her a wink.

"It's going to be okay. Is that your father?" He nodded toward a fit older man who seemed to be holding court across the pool.

"Yep. And look, Mom's already in a state of blessed boredom." Her mother sat at a table with an equally bored looking friend. They were both sipping champagne and shaking their heads at anyone who walked by. "Mother believes in never having a facial expression. Botox was her salvation."

Will frowned. "She's had way too much of it. And what's wrong with her eyebrows?"

"Ah, the great brow lift of '02. They tweaked it a bit too much and it won't go down now. She thinks it makes her look intellectual."

"You're kidding."

"Welcome to my family." She glanced around at the usual suspects. "That's Uncle Andrew on my mother's side. He recently got out of jail for defrauding investors to the tune of a hundred million. He did a total of six months due to his incredibly good lawyer, and now he's shopping a book based on the 'enlightenment' he found in prison. He's talking to my Great Aunt Vespa, who is being investigated for having not one, not two, but thirteen undocumented workers living in her pool house. Yes, she had one poor girl who did nothing but take care of her hair and nails. I don't know what she did with the rest of them. I think she tried to tell them one was a chef, but I happen to know she doesn't eat. If you look to your left, those are my cousins, Violet and Meryl. Between the two, they've gone through five husbands, each older and richer than the last. No children though. That would ruin their figures. I've heard a rumor they're doing a show next year called The Real Cock-Sucking, Gold-Diggers of Malibu. Or something like that."

"Are you sure it's not housewives?"

She rolled her eyes. "Trust me. Those two are professionals. There's nothing stay-at-home about them." She flipped them the finger because they were already talking behind their hands, and she knew exactly who they were talking about.

Will grabbed her hand and his eyes narrowed. "No. Bad girl. Down."

Asshole. But he'd made her smile. "I'm not allowed to bite then?"

"Or bark." He brought the hand to his mouth and kissed her middle finger before easing it down. "We'll get through this my way and that means you are going to play nice. Can we do that? And I promise when you turn the other cheek because these people don't matter and you're better than them, I'll give you a treat. I'll start carrying chocolates around in my pocket."

He'd changed into slacks, a dress shirt, and a sport coat. His hair was still slightly wet from taking over her shower. That had been one of the five times since the damn plane that he'd decided to show her his deep affection. She couldn't help but laugh at him. "I am not your puppy, Will. We are not going there."

He'd been teasing her about puppy play. She was so not tempted.

He leaned over and whispered in her ear. "But then I could pet you and rub your sweet belly, and when you're good, I could give you a treat to lick."

Yeah, she could imagine exactly what he would offer her. "But I'm a puppy who buries her treats, babe."

He sent her a wounded look. "That's rude. Bad puppy. Puppy wants a spanking." He leaned over and kissed her. "Puppy's going to get one."

"Well, that looks like it worked." Chris strode up looking spectacularly handsome in slacks and a polo. He also looked like he hadn't spent the day being penetrated by a horny doctor. He had a glow about him that spoke of a day in the sun. "The evil twins are shooting you nasty looks."

She glanced over and sure enough, they were staring at Will and then back at her like they were trying to figure out what had happened to the universe that she'd landed such a hottie.

Her first instinct was to shout out something like "look what my porn money bought," but she decided Will would likely view that as misbehaving. She was going to be a good puppy. For now.

Not that she was going to do the puppy thing. Not at all. Most likely.

She settled for what she hoped was a serene smile.

"Oh, shit, who did you kill?" Chris asked, his eyes wide.

Will waved him off. "She didn't kill anyone. She's taking a ladylike approach to her relatives."

Chris stared at her like she'd grown horns. "What kind of drugs did you give her and can I get some?"

"Jerk." She was sure her good behavior would throw Chris for a loop, but she was willing to try it Will's way. She usually attended these events with full on rebellion and defiance, but he was right. They weren't worth the effort. She smiled her cousins' way.

"Oh, god. Are you going to kill Violet?" Amy was standing in front of her, shaking her head in horror.

Did no one really believe she could smile simply because she was happy? "I'm not going to kill anyone. I'm happy to see you. How's the corporate world treating you?"

Her baby sister was a VP at Slaten, and from what Bridget had heard, she was one of the smartest young executives in the business. With a slender form and chicly cut black hair, she could pass for a model, but there was no doubt about her brainpower. She'd graduated from Wharton School of Business. She hugged Bridget warmly and then kissed Chris on the cheek. "It would be wonderful if I liked my boss."

Their father. The bastard. "Why don't you quit? Why are you doing this? Amy, we can get on a plane today and I'll help you until you find your feet."

"We can find you a place to live in Dallas, and I have no doubt you can easily get a job there," Chris said.

Her sister had a great resume. She could do it. It would be hard for Amy to leave everything behind, but Bridget had done it.

Amy shook her head. "I wish. If I leave, who's going to protect those workers? They've been like family to us over the years, and Dad will fire off the experienced workers and swindle them out of their pensions. You know it as well as I do. I managed to keep him from shipping everything over to China last year. No. I have plans. I have to be patient and let them happen. Now, hello, you gorgeous hunk of fake, soon-to-be brother-in-law. Damn, but you are fine."

She was grinning up at Will, who seemed to take the compliment in stride.

"Thank you. I try to live up to Bridget's standards," Will said.

That wouldn't be hard. He'd bathed. That was a step up from her last do-nothing boyfriend. Yeah, she didn't mention that either. She was really maturing. It was a good thing.

"Now, you have to meet my Frankie. He's the sweetest thing ever and I adore him." She took Bridget's hand and started to lead her toward the bar. Will and Chris followed.

An almost blindingly gorgeous man turned and smiled. He was at least six foot three, with a movie star face and the most perfect lips she'd ever seen on a man. He was dressed casually, but nothing could hide the lean strength of his body. He took off his perfectly paired aviators and Bridget nearly got lost in his blue eyes.

"You must be Bridget." Even his voice was perfect. Lyrical. Musical.

She stood there staring at him.

Will elbowed her. "Have you lost use of your tongue, sweetheart? Maybe I should check you out. You could have a neurological problem." He held his hand out. "Since my lovely fiancée seems to have lost the power of speech, I'm Will Daley. Nice to meet you."

Frankie held out a hand and they shook.

Why was she suddenly thinking about an MMF? They would look so pretty together.

Chris leaned over and whispered in her ear. "Dibs."

She turned on him. They often had the same ideas for stories because great minds really did think alike, but he was not taking this one. No way. Will was her damn Dom and she kind of almost owned Frankie I'm-a-Love-God by way of marriage. "You don't get dibs on this. I own this."

He grinned. "Nope. I called dibs. I already have the story in my head."

"Do I even want to know what you two are talking about?" Will asked.

"No," they managed to say in perfect harmony.

She got her bearings back. Frankie was a gorgeous god of a man, but she kind of preferred Will's broader body and more masculine face. It was good to know the man could get jealous though. She held out a hand. "It's nice to meet you. Might I say welcome to the family?"

His hand was warm in hers. "Thank you. I'm madly in love with your sister. Hell, I'd marry her for her handbag collection alone. And that hair. You look gorgeous, darling." He turned to Chris, his eyes boldly running the length of Chris's body with obvious appreciation. "And hello. Who is this?"

What? Delicious boy had set off her gaydar. Hard. Like lights swirling, why can't everyone else hear that siren blaring hard.

Will had a smirk on his face that let Bridget know he had a gaydar, too.

Shit. Her sister was marrying a gay dude. Which would be totally and completely fine if she happened to be packing a penis. Which she wasn't.

Chris's eyes went wide as he shook hands with Frankie. "Chris Roberts."

"You're one of the writers," Frankie said with obvious glee. "I am so excited about sitting down with you two and talking about where you get your ideas. I love creative types."

Amy put a hand on Frankie's perfectly pressed shirtsleeve. "Babe, there's my cousin. He has a voting share, so we need to go make nice. Bridget, let's catch up in a bit, okay? I'm so happy you're here. Love you, sis."

She and Frankie made their way to cousin Lance, who was one of their more reasonable relatives.

"Holy shit, Bridget. He is one of my people," Chris said, still watching the couple.

"Damn straight he is. And by straight I mean gay. That dude is totally gay." There was a wealth of satisfaction in Will's voice.

"Does she know? Oh god. She can't know. Shit. I have to be the bad guy again." She was always, always put in this position. "How am I going to tell my sister that she's marrying a gay guy? Why does he want to marry her?"

"Apparently he likes her handbags," Chris offered.

"Bridget, you came." Her mother was moving toward them with that lazy stride she used when she was drunk. Which was almost always.

She turned her cheek up and allowed her mother to do that fakey-fake air kiss thing she did to everyone. "I did, indeed."

"It's nice to see you looking so…healthy, dear." Her mother sighed. "And your hair. It's grown out. It's very retro. This must be the doctor fiancé." She held her hand out toward Chris. She'd met him once before, but it didn't surprise Bridget at all that her mom didn't remember.

Will stepped in. "No. That would be me."

Her mother's weird eyebrow managed to go even higher. "You're with Bridget?"

Well, the hits kept coming, didn't they? Healthy was her mother's version of fat and retro meant she should cut her hair since she was over thirty and in her mother's mind, only little girls and supermodels had long hair. Now dear mother was shocked that the hot doc was her date.

Will slid an arm around her waist and smiled readily. "Yes. I'm so glad to finally meet her family."

Her mother sighed and then she was off again, likely in search of another bottle of Pinot.

Chris shook his head. "She's as sweet as ever."

Will shook his head. "Did I miss something?"

"I don't think he speaks our language." She could explain to him that her mother had insulted her, but she was trying to stay positive. "It's okay. Hey, is that Mitch? What's he doing here?"

Surprise registered on Will's face as he stepped away. "No idea. Do you want to go say hi with me?"

She shook her head. "Go on. I'm going to get a drink and start trying to figure out how to tell Amy her stud isn't interested in her plumbing situation." Will walked away and she turned to Chris. "He could be bi, right?"

"Oh, I doubt it, honey." He kissed her cheek. "I'm going to go get Jeremy. He sent me a text saying he's in the lobby and can't find the place. I'll introduce him to Frankie and see if he agrees, but I think you're screwed."

Because her sister wouldn't ever be if she married Frankie.

She walked up to the bar. Alcohol was so needed. "Could I get a rum and diet? Heavy on the rum, please."

The bartender nodded.

"So you decided to come," a low voice said behind her.

Her father. She was going to be calm. She was going to be a lady. She forced herself to turn. Her father was standing there in what had to be a three thousand dollar Italian suit and Ferragamo loafers. Amid all the lush relaxation of the islands, he still looked like a captain of industry, but then image was everything to George Slaten. Bridget couldn't miss the way he took in her maxi dress and sandals with a frown. "Yes. I wouldn't miss Amy's wedding for the world."

He gestured to the bartender, who immediately pulled out the good Scotch. "She's a good daughter and a fine executive, if she would just get those stupid notions out of her head. She needs to nurture the bottom line, not those idiots who are always looking for a handout."

Her dad was a giver. "I believe she would call them employees, Dad."

He shrugged. "They're replaceable, but she forgets that. So are you still peddling smut?"

Ah, so the pleasantries were over. "Are you still screwing the general public six ways from Sunday?" Damn it. She was supposed to be ladylike and turn the other cheek. She'd promised. "I am still writing if that's what you're asking. I make a good living at it, too."

"Enough to buy yourself a boyfriend, I see." He nodded to the place where Will was talking to Mitch. Ian Taggart and Jake Dean had joined them. Jake had what looked like a baby carrier strapped to his chest. Yep. Tristan's fat baby legs were hanging down.

She was going to take the high road. Will was right. Her father wasn't worth fighting with. Not when she could get baby cuddles from Tristan and hunk cuddles from Will. Maybe if his arms were around her she could forget she was surrounded by sharks. She picked up her drink. "If you'll excuse me…"

Her father reached out and grabbed her arms. "No, I will not. I want to talk to you. I know you came out here to fuck up your sister's wedding, but I'm going to stop you here and now."

She really hated him. "Why would you want her to marry him? He can't love her. Not the way she deserves."

"I don't give a crap about your sister's love life. I do, however, give a shit about my business. You see that shiny prick over there? The one your sister is marrying? His family owns one of California's largest real estate companies. When they get married, we're going to merge and Slaten is going to have the final piece to the puzzle we've needed. Our stock will soar and then I'll sell this fucking company and be done with it."

He wanted to sell the company their grandfather and great grandfather had built? Her granddad had been one of the only members of the family she and Amy could stand. She often thought they'd survived their childhoods because of long stretches spent with their grandparents. "I'll tell Amy. How could you do this? That company is her birthright."

"That company is mine to do with as I please. I'm going to get everything I can out of it and then retire. Amy can inherit what I don't manage to spend, but don't think you're going to get a dime. I told you when you walked out of the house that you wouldn't get a single cent from me. You made your choice."

Because she hadn't been willing to fall in line. She'd never regretted it once. She'd held down two jobs until she'd started making enough to support herself with her writing. She'd built her life and it was good, but Amy had always loved the company. Amy had been preparing to take over the company from the day she'd been born. "I'll stop it. The only reason she's stayed with the company is to protect the workers. She'll walk away from this wedding. She won't do this."

Her father leaned in, his voice taking a distinctly nasty tone. "You could tell her. But then I'll make sure your boy toy over there doesn't work again. Did you think I wouldn't have time to check him out? I work fast, sweetheart. I have connections at the hospital where he works. It's owned by a large conglomerate, one whose CEO happens to be at this wedding. How is he going to take it when I start talking about your boy's sexual proclivities? Did you think I wouldn't know about that? I'm not surprised you turned out to be such a slut. Did you know his mother's in prison for dealing drugs? Do you think he's involved in that, too? I bet the hospital will wonder. How about the fact that he was involved with a serial killer? He's done a fine job of keeping that out of the press, but I assure you I can make it national news. Brain doc doesn't have a brain in his head. How's that for a headline?"

Anger flashed through her system. "He was not. He had nothing to do with those killings."

He shrugged as if he couldn't care less. "The press might see it that way. Or they might be open to questions about it. All I'm saying is it would be in his best interest if your sister's wedding runs smoothly."

His way or the highway. Or in this case, his way or Will lost his job and got humiliated in the press.

She knew exactly how he felt. Will was private. He would be horrified to have his life spread out like that.

Anger sat in her gut, but she nodded. She'd gotten Will into this. She couldn't let him get caught up in her father's crap. "I guess I should wish her a happy wedding then, shouldn't I?"

"You always were a smart girl. Never used it much, but smart. Now get out of my sight. You're here for your sister. The rest of the family would rather you didn't exist."

She nodded and walked away, but not toward Will. She headed for the beach.

It would be good to remind herself that she was alone. Always alone.

* * * *

"What kind of protection is that thing supposed to be?" Taggart was asking Jacob Dean as Will approached. He was staring at the baby carrier.

"Well, for one thing, it doesn't let him slide to the ground," Dean replied.

Taggart took a swig of the beer he was holding. "It does nothing to stop a bullet."

Dean rolled his eyes and he patted his son's back. "No. Surprisingly my baby carrier isn't made of Kevlar."

"And that is where you've chosen poorly, my friend. Think about it. Baby would be protected and your whole chest area suddenly isn't a big open target. I'm just saying why can't it serve two purposes. That baby Charlie's carrying is getting the full package. She's thinking jogging stroller, but I think we should go with bulletproof all the way." Taggart nodded. "Daley, how's it going? I see Bridget hasn't killed you yet. I lost that bet."

"You owe me twenty," Dean replied.

"No. Bridget and I get along fine. Mitch, what are you doing here?" Will asked, staring at his friend, who looked more casual than he could remember seeing him.

Mitch pointed Taggart's way. "The big guy called and asked me to come along. Apparently he finally met Slaten and now he's trying to find a way out of this contract."

Taggart shook his head. "No. I'm fine with the contract. But I'm probably going to do something really horrible to the man, and I thought my attorney should witness the crime."

"Actually, that's a bad idea," Mitch admitted. "I shouldn't be witness to any crimes you might commit. But I will look through those documents you asked me to look into. I'm going through some of the corporate bylaws and structure for Bridget's sister. She had some questions. Ian had concerns and at the last minute, a couple of seats opened up on the plane. Any idea how that happened?"

"Hey, I wanted some alone time." It had gone spectacularly well. He was looking forward to getting her alone again. Once the family cleared out, they would have a whole week to themselves. Now that he thought about it, he should propose more than a month for their next contract. They could safely sign a contract for six months. That seemed reasonable.

"It's a good thing Mitch is here," Taggart said. "Bridget's dad is such an asshole that I think I really am going to need a lawyer." He sobered a little. "Keep her away from him, man. He's toxic. He talks about both his daughters like they're property to be dispensed with, and I won't even go into the man's sexual proclivities."

"His sexual proclivities?"

He shook his head as though shaking some nasty image out of his brain. "Hey, I had Li shadow him after we signed him up. I should have done it before, but he kind of dazzled me with the whole signing bonus deal. I got mouths to feed. Li needed a new partner and damn Damon hired some sad-sack Russian. I swear every ex-agent with a sob story shows up on my doorstep."

He did not need to listen to Taggart complain. The man could do it for hours. "Back to Bridget's dad."

"Hey, I have a conscience. I also have a couple of hours of tape on the son of a bitch if we ever need it." Taggart shook his head. "Trust me. I know who has the best odds for filing crazy lawsuits and not paying up. I have to cut that shit off at the pass."

"Mitch?" a familiar female voice said.

Will turned slowly, hoping and praying that he was mistaken. "Laurel?"

His eldest sister was holding two glasses of wine and gave him a sheepish grin. "Hey, big brother."

"Hello, sister. Want to explain why you're here." He suddenly figured it out and turned on his best friend. "Are you fucking kidding me?"

"I don't think he knew they were screwing," Taggart whispered to Dean.

"Definitely not," Dean agreed.

It was good to know they were entertaining someone. "Your opinions are not needed."

"Don't think of them as opinions. Merely reactions to the show, buddy," Taggart replied with a grin. "Continue on. You should definitely mention the fact that Mitch has gone through like five wives."

Laurel rolled her eyes and got in between Will and Mitch. She proved her moxie by pointing a finger the big boys' way. "You two, stop being jerks around the baby. Mitch has only been married twice. He has terrible taste in women. And I'm here because I'm working for him. He hired me on two weeks ago."

Yeah, Will bet he had. He loved Mitch like a brother, but the man was known for going through women, and he didn't want one of those women to be his sister. "I'll get you another job."

Just for a second, a flash of rage went across Mitch's face. It was quickly subdued and replaced with his usual devil-may-care vibe, but Will hadn't missed it. No matter what he said, Mitch was interested in Laurel.

Will wasn't sure how he felt about that.

"Gentlemen, if you'll excuse me. I need to talk to my brother for a moment." Laurel gripped his elbow and he found himself being hauled away.

"I'm only watching out for you."

Laurel's jaw became a stubborn line as she glared up at him. He might have gotten Bridget happy with him, but he seemed doomed to forever have a female pissed off at him. "He is your friend and you hurt him. You will back off and let me handle my own business. I am an adult. I've gotten through college and I'm ready to make my own decisions. Is that understood?"

127

She needed to understand a few things about Mitch. "He's interested in you. Not as a secretary."

"Good because he's not stupid and backward enough to call me a secretary. I'm an office manager. I have a business degree. His books are horrible. He's got a brilliant mind and not an organizational skill in his body."

He was going to have to be really clear with her. "Laurel, he's interested in you as a woman."

"Again with the good. I'm interested in him as a man. Now if you'll give me a few tips on how to get that man in bed, I would appreciate it because he is proving to be very difficult."

He couldn't help but wince. "I did not need to hear that."

"Then you shouldn't have butted in where you don't belong," Laurel shot back. "I understand that Mitch has been divorced a couple of times. The man has had to start from scratch twice. I'm fairly certain that's why he's so skittish."

"He's also into some hardcore hobbies." He didn't want to go into what Mitch needed sexually. He'd talked to his sisters about going to clubs, but he wasn't going into details.

Laurel crossed her arms over her chest and sent him a pointed stare. "That's the pot calling the kettle black. If you're talking about the BDSM stuff, you shouldn't judge, big brother. And I'm cool with it. Reading Bridget's books have opened me up to the idea that I might enjoy submitting to the right man in the bedroom."

He put his hands over his ears. "Oh, god. Don't. Please. Wait, you've been reading Bridget's books?"

"Duh. I was reading her before you started dating her. I love her stuff. She's funny and she has a lot to say about what a woman deserves. I guess it's about what people deserve out of a relationship."

"Orgasms, right? I mean she writes about single women with multiple men."

Laurel shook her head. "It's a metaphor, dummy. All of those men are actually aspects of one. At least that's how I see it. I can't explain it. You have to read it. And you're a horrible boyfriend for not reading her books."

"I'm not really..."

She held a hand up, stopping him from finishing his sentence. "Don't say it. Don't say you're not her boyfriend, Will."

But he wasn't and it looked like he was going to have to explain. "I'm her Dom and you obviously know what that means."

"I know that it's your way of distancing yourself and it makes me sad."

What was she talking about? "I'm not distancing myself. I'm quite close to her."

"Have you told her you love her?" Laurel asked.

A weariness settled over him. He thought this restlessness would fade when Bridget agreed to simply be with him, but it was stronger than ever. "You know how I feel about that word."

"Yes, I do know and that makes me sad. I've thought about this a lot and I have something to say to you. Lisa and Lila and I have been talking about it. I think you have a twisted version of the word."

He was really ready to give in so he didn't need to have this argument with the women in his life. "It's only a word, Laurel, and if it bothers everyone so freaking much, I'll use it. It doesn't have to mean anything."

"Because it didn't mean anything when Mom used it. Will, I think when you hear that word, you still see her."

"Don't give me that bullshit." He didn't need another Kai.

"It's true," Laurel replied with passion. Her voice went low but he could hear the force of will there. "You think I don't remember. I remember how she would tell us she loved us. Especially when she was high. She would bring her boyfriends home and she loved them, too. She would call from jail and coax you into picking her up when we got older. She did it by telling you she loved you. It was just a word for her and you've put that definition on it. But I have a different definition and I wish you could see it my way."

This whole conversation made him uncomfortable. It was better to leave the past behind, but he needed to know why she saw things differently than he did. "We grew up in the same household. We should have the same definition."

She shook her head. "But I knew I was loved. Do you know what I think of when I hear the word? I think of a twelve-year-old boy trying to figure out how to do my pigtails so the other kids wouldn't make fun of me at school. I think of an eighteen-year-old who could have gone to any school he wanted, but he stayed close to home so he could raise three teenagers. When I think of love, I think of my brother because I always knew I was loved. I wish you did. I wish you knew how much we love you, Will. I wish you could see how much that woman you're dating…excuse me, dominating or something…is capable of loving you."

"I know you care about me." Maybe she was right because it really was hard to say the freaking word.

She shook her head and got into his space. "No. I love you. I love you so much. I want everything that is good and right in the world for you. So do Lila and Lisa. And I think Bridget might be the woman who can take care of you."

"I don't need to be taken care of."

"Don't you? Don't you deserve it?"

And hadn't he already slipped into that kind of partnership with Bridget? He woke her up when he had to go to the hospital, something he would never have done with his other lovers. He'd been able to read the charts on his tablet and be more prepared for the surgery because Bridget had driven him. He'd told himself it was all right because Bridget's work was flexible and there was valet service at their building so she would be safe. He'd desperately needed the help, but he wouldn't have asked anyone but her. Because deep down he trusted her. He trusted her with herself. She wouldn't take crazy chances. She was infinitely competent. She didn't want or need to be treated like a finely made piece of glass. She was a magnificently made woman, and he was going to lose her.

She wouldn't stay with a man who couldn't love her. Not forever.

He had to enjoy the time he had. The now. He had to hold on to the now.

He kissed his sister on the forehead. "You be careful with Mitch. He's a good guy, but those two women damn near broke him in ways that have nothing to do with his finances."

She gave him a long hug. "I'll be careful. And if I ever manage to get him to really look at me, I'll be careful with him. Try to think about what I said."

"I will." He doubted he could do anything else because he was worried now that no matter what kind of contract he wrapped her in, he still wouldn't be enough for her.

Chapter Ten

T wo days later, Will watched Bridget. She looked gorgeous in her sarong and sandals, as the light of the fire from the torches seemed to caress her skin. The night was warm and she was surrounded by friends. None of the family had come to this luau prepared for the bride and groom. From what he understood, George Slaten was busy with business contacts and Bridget's mom was busy with a bottle of Malbec.

There was soft Hawaiian music playing and the roast pig smelled fabulous. Bridget had carried baby Tristan around for a while, showing him the sights, and for those moments she seemed truly happy.

Bridget liked kids. She was going to want kids.

Fuck. Did he want kids?

All he knew was that the thought of Bridget having someone else's baby got his guts in a knot.

Laurel smiled and sat down next to Bridget, who seemed to be on her way to being her new best friend. Why wasn't she smiling? She hadn't really smiled at him for two days. Not since he'd found her walking on the beach by herself.

Something had happened and she wouldn't talk about it. All she would tell him was she'd decided that her sister was an adult and they shouldn't butt in.

Something had gone terribly wrong because Bridget always butted in. Always.

Since that day on the beach, the only time he felt close to her was when they were making love. Only then would she soften and wrap her arms around him and give everything to him.

Was she starting to guess that he was a bad bet?

"Doctor Daley?" a voice asked.

He turned and saw Frankie standing there in all his golden boy glory. Yeah, it was a good thing the dude was probably gay because Will had not liked how Bridget's chin had dropped at the very sight of him. It wasn't like the man was that good looking. Surely he had flaws. Somewhere.

Even Will had to admit he kind of liked the dude. He'd been a perfect gentleman around Bridget, even getting her to laugh from time to time.

Will forced himself to nod. "Hey, how's it going?"

"Beautifully so far. Only a few days more. Can I talk to you for a moment?"

Great. Will followed him and found himself led to a far corner of the park that overlooked the ocean. The sounds of the waves should have been soothing, but he had a feeling this conversation wasn't going to be at all pleasant. "What do you want to talk about?"

"Bridget and Amy. The family situation. I need to understand where you fit, Daley. Amy hasn't said much, but I do understand that until a few days ago, I'd never heard your name and now you're engaged to Bridget. I want to know if this is one of Amy's schemes. She's quite good at them."

If Amy hadn't told him anything, then he didn't need to know. "My relationship with Bridget is none of your business."

"I disagree," Frankie replied. "I'm Amy's fiancé. I love her quite dearly. If you're some sort of rent-a-hunk himbo here to take Bridget for all she's worth, then I'm going to have to shut you down. I'm not going to allow anyone to hurt Amy, and Amy would be hurt if her sister was. I'm afraid I'll have to be quite firm on this matter."

"You're really in love with Amy?"

He turned, the hint of an enigmatic smile on his face. "I'm quite devoted to her. I have been since we met a few months ago. You know how you meet a person and realize very quickly you have a connection?"

He'd known from the moment he saw Bridget that he wanted her. He'd known within days of sleeping with her that he needed her. "I guess I do."

Frankie sighed as he stared out over the ocean. "I love Amy, but as you've already figured out, there are many kinds of love."

"So you admit she's not your type." He still wasn't so sure Bridget was right about not talking to her sister, but who was he to complain? He'd tried to butt into his own sister's love life and Mitch still seemed stiff and awkward around him. He'd fucked things up with his best friend and almost alienated his sister.

Frankie shook his head. "She's everyone's type and that's all I'll say on the matter. Now, I would like to know how much it's going to cost me to get you out of Bridget's life."

Okay. Now he didn't like the man very much. "There is not enough money in the world."

Frankie finally turned and gave Will an assessing look. "I'm thinking there is. She doesn't have any, you know. I mean she's got what she makes from her writing, and that's not an insubstantial amount, but it's nothing compared to the Slaten fortune. How about I pay you a hundred thousand? That should cover your medical school loans and leave you with a little something left over. I'm sure if you stayed with Bridget for several years you could amass that much, but now you can have it all in one go. And you can find another target."

Will's blood pressure ticked up. He'd managed to keep Bridget calm for days. He wasn't about to cause a scene himself. "I am going to forgo the pleasure of beating you senseless, you piece of shit. I'm going to do it because Bridget would be upset, but if you ever talk to me again, I don't know what I'll do. Bridget is mine. Mine, do you understand? And no one in this god-forsaken family of hers is going to come between us. I've been here for exactly two days and I already know every single one of you is rotten to the core. I have zero idea how that woman came from this family. She's worth a hundred of you."

A slow smile spread across Frankie's face. "Is that right?"

"Yes, that's right." He finally got it. He finally figured out why her mother calling her healthy had bugged her. "Healthy means fat. That bitch. She stood right in front of me and called her daughter fat."

"Mother Slaten is very good at that," Frankie replied as though it should have been obvious. "Not much good at anything else."

Now he could see that every single woman in her family, with the exception of her sister, had subtly insulted her. "She's gorgeous, and I won't listen to anyone who says otherwise."

"She is a stunning woman. She's almost as beautiful as her sister. So George didn't send you I take it." Frankie took a deep breath. "I'm glad to hear that. I've been working myself up to this scene for days."

"Bridget's dad? Why do you think he sent me? Why would he send me?"

"Well, I discovered a connection to you a few days before we flew out here. You see, I snoop. A lot. It's one of my hobbies. George has a file on you. I wasn't able to read it, but he keeps files on all his employees. I was worried he'd sent you in to handle Bridget. It would be exactly like him to send his own man to ensure the prodigal daughter's return didn't disrupt his plans. I assume Bridget's going to attempt to talk Amy out of marrying me. George won't let that happen."

Will shook his head, trying to take it in. This family's intrigues astonished him. He'd figured out rapidly that they very rarely said what they meant. It was all a dance of subtle insults and backhanded compliments. "I hadn't met the man before dinner the other night. Bridget introduced me, but she got us out of his line of fire really quickly. I'm not a plant. We had mutual friends and I pursued her until I ran her to ground."

"So you are engaged?"

"Of course we are." He wasn't going to give up the game at this point.

Frankie chuckled. "You're a horrible liar. Let me guess. My Amy got sick of her cousins talking about Bridget. She had too much wine and announced that Bridget was dating a hot guy. Oh, but Amy never does things halfway. She likely said Bridget was getting married, too."

It was obvious that Frankie knew his fiancée well. "I think you should talk to Amy about that."

Frankie tipped his head as though agreeing to the point. "Well, obviously I apologize for trying to buy you off and for suggesting that you might be a paid escort."

"Hey, I've never been accused of prostitution before. It's a new experience. So that begs the question of why Slaten has a file on me."

"More than likely because he was trying to get leverage on you. It's what he likes to do. He's not as clever as he thinks he is though. And he definitely likes to underestimate the people around him. Especially his daughters."

So Bridget's dad had been digging up dirt. He would find quite a bit. He could take all that dirty laundry right to Bridget and lay it out.

And Bridget would defend him to the death. She could find out all his secrets and she would still be by his side. She'd accepted that his mother was in prison. She'd accepted that he'd grown up in a disgusting trailer and that he'd been an idiot about Starr. Would she come to accept that he wouldn't love her? Eventually, perhaps. He could see it quite plainly. She would sign the contract for a month and then he could easily shift them into a longer-term contract. He could make the argument that they didn't need two places, or better yet, that they would really do better with a house.

He would ply her with affection and sex and his special brand of dominance and she would give up on those dreams of having a man who returned her love.

What did she mean when she used the word love? It was a stupid word that meant absolutely nothing to him, but Laurel's speech kept playing around in his head. Words could have many meanings. He needed to figure out what Bridget meant by love because he was rapidly coming to the conclusion that she was as necessary for his happiness as breathing.

"You say you love Amy. What do you mean by that?"

Frankie stared at him for a moment. "Mean?"

"What does love mean to you? I…I don't get it. You're not sleeping with her. If I'm wrong, I apologize, but I'm trying to figure something out."

"You're not wrong. Amy and I don't sleep together, but we are an odd form of soul mates. I think the idea that we only get one is wrong. At least I hope it is. I think maybe we go through life finding these people who hold little pieces of our soul. Sometimes you find a big chunk and I think that might be what we call love."

He growled under his breath, frustration taking over. "I don't get the metaphysical shit."

"All right. You're a literal guy. Uhm, I love Amy because she accepts me. I can be exactly who I am around her. I don't have to pretend the way I do around others. She's a safe place for me. When we first met, well, let's say I wasn't in a good place. I'm here today because of that woman. Whatever happens, she's my friend for life. Do you love Bridget? I asked and you didn't answer."

He hated that question and yet he answered because Frankie had been open with him. "I don't know. I want her."

"That's a good start. You don't have to know now. She seems happy."

Yeah, Frankie didn't know her. Bridget was saying all the right things, but Will knew what she looked like when she was truly happy. He let it go because there was no point.

"Hey, buddy, you seem to be out of those coconut cookies. I know that sounds sad, but I have a woman who can't drink for another six months, so I get her whatever she tells me to. Who do I need to pay to get me about two dozen or so of those suckers?" Ian Taggart asked, his big body blocking the light from the party.

Taggart was a man who knew how to get what he wanted. He was a man who always had a plan. Will was fairly certain his plans had plans. What would a man like Taggart do if his wife's family was making her miserable? If Taggart's wife's father had dug up dirt on him to ruin their relationship, what would he do?

"I'll speak to the caterer," Frankie was saying. "I noticed your wife seems to like coconut. I'll have them bring out the ice cream early."

Taggart would already have a plan in place.

"Thanks. Make it a lot though. She really likes ice cream," Taggart said.

Will remembered their conversation from a few nights before. Taggart did have a plan in place.

Frankie nodded and left, but Will stopped Taggart as he turned.

"Ian, I need a favor."

Taggart's whole face turned stony. "You can't have those cookies. Seriously, don't get between Charlie and her chosen snack food."

"I need to see that footage you have of George Slaten. I think I want to buy it."

Taggart's brows rose. "Why?"

"Because he's going to try to come between me and Bridget, and I won't let it happen. Because if he says one more thing to make her sad, I swear I will kill the man."

Taggart's lips tugged up. "Now you're talking. Come on. I've got it on my computer. I've been dying to use it on that asshole, but Charlie told me I had to play fair. Really, this is a gift to me. How about I charge you five bucks? Five bucks and now you're a client. I'm protecting you from Slaten."

"Isn't that a conflict of interest?"

"Nah, I have zero interest in Slaten. He's an asshole. You see, all these rules just make things hard. Besides, that's what Mitch is here for. When Slaten sues us, Mitch gets to work. Everyone's happy." Taggart slapped him on the back. "Come on. I'll show you what I've got and you'll see why I've been dying to use it. Why is it always the self-righteous pricks who turn out to be complete perverts? You know it gives the rest of us a bad name. Own your perversion, dude."

He followed Taggart, happy to at least have a plan.

* * * *

Bridget felt weary as she entered the room. Her sister was getting married tomorrow night and she was in a corner. If she talked to her about it, Will got hurt. If she didn't, her sister did.

She'd thought about it all throughout the luau. She'd sat and watched her friends and wondered if there was a way out.

It made her tired and heartsick, and she was beginning to think it was better to be alone.

"Do you want something to drink, sweetheart?" Will asked as he locked the door.

There wasn't enough wine in the world. She shook her head. "No, I think I'm going to go to bed. Tomorrow's a big day."

She would watch her sister walk down the aisle and then spend a week alone with Will and then what? She knew it was stupid, knew she should accept the pleasure the moment could bring, but damn it, she would always be worrying about the future. It sat there in her gut like a hunger that wouldn't go away. She loved him. There wasn't a point in fooling herself about how deep she was in. She could even accept that he didn't love her, but it hurt to be around him knowing the truth.

She'd smiled and tried to get along with everyone for his sake, but she felt battered. It was like loving him had made the walls she'd built crumble and she had no more defenses. The only times she felt good were when she was in his arms, when she told him she loved him and all he could ever tell her was he was "glad."

Her heart thudded in her chest and she fought back tears. Too much. Too much emotion. She needed to be alone.

"Hey, Bridget, come here. I want to talk to you."

She stopped at the bedroom door. "Not tonight."

He put a hand on her arm lightly, turning her to face him. "Yes. Tonight."

"Don't push me." She didn't need to fight with him. She would say things she didn't mean. He'd taken down all her walls and if he pushed her, she would fight dirty. "I don't want to talk tonight."

His face softened. "Sweetheart, it's nothing bad. I want to talk to you about a longer-term contract. Look, I know the last few days have been rough on you, but you've come through it all with grace. You've been wonderful. I think we should consider signing a year-long contract."

"Is that some treat for not being myself? I get to stay with you for a year?" Bitterness welled.

His brows came together in obvious consternation. "Bridget, that's not what I meant. I don't have a problem with who you are. You're passionate. I like that about you. But you don't have to fight every single person you meet. Especially not when the fight isn't worth it."

He was so reasonable. Unfortunately, she wasn't in a reasonable mood. "So what you're saying is if I'm a good sub who never yells or fights, you'll like who I am. That's great, Will."

"Tell me what's wrong." His voice had taken on a soothing tone and that annoyed her.

"You really want to know?"

He sighed but didn't back away. "I would like to know the truth and not whatever bullshit is about to come out of your mouth because you're mad at your family and you're ready to take it out on me. I'll take some of it. I'm the one who set the rules about your behavior. If it helps, I can easily see why you would want to run through these people like a bull on stampede, but that won't help your sister and then you'll feel guilty. Why don't you come here and let me hold you for a while? We can sit and talk."

He wasn't listening to a word she was saying. "I don't want to talk. I wanted to go to bed. Now I kind of want to get everything over with."

"Everything? That sounds a bit dramatic."

Of course. She was a drama queen. She'd heard that one before. "God, you're condescending sometimes."

"I'll admit to that. What's this really about?"

It looked like they were going to have this out. He wouldn't back down. He wouldn't let her go to bed so she could talk herself into staying.

She was in a corner and she did what she always did when she was in a corner. She lashed out. "You. It's about you. You and your fucking contracts. I'm not signing another one. I'm not staying here with you. I'm leaving tomorrow night."

His jaw tightened and he turned around, striding to the bar. "All right, we'll go home if that's what you want."

Now he was purposefully misunderstanding her. "Without you. I'm leaving without you."

His hands came out and he leaned on the bar, his head slumping down like he was too tired to hold it up a second longer. "Sweetheart, don't do this. Don't say a bunch of things you'll have to take back later."

Her first instinct was to go to him, to soothe him, but that would land her in more trouble. He was tempting, so tempting, but she had to be strong. "Because of course I don't know what I'm doing. Because I should take what you're willing to give me and be happy I have a man for a while."

"That's your family talking." He was still using that reasonable tone that set her on edge. "They're toxic, but we'll be away from them soon."

There was piece of her that knew he was right, but she was on a path now. She wanted to have it done so she could go back into her shell and never fucking come out again. "It doesn't matter. Will, I can't be with a man who is never going to love me. I know you don't believe this, but at some point in time you're going to find the woman you do love and I can't watch that. I can't just be some chick you spend time with until the real one comes along. I love you. I love you so much I ache with it. I love you so much I would do anything for you. I can't stay with you when you don't feel the same way."

His hands became fists and he slammed them down on the bar, making the glasses jump. "Oh, for fuck's sake. Fine. I love you. I love you, Bridget. I'll say it."

She held her ground as he turned around, anger and frustration in his eyes. She was pissed off, too. "But you don't mean it."

He stalked toward her. "You only seem to give a shit about the words. It doesn't matter to you that I'm willing to promise that I'll be good to you and I'll be faithful. All that matters is some words that anyone can say."

Her whole body tensed. Now that she was in the moment, she didn't want to be here, but it was something to be survived. She had to get through this so she could crawl into a cave and hide. "There is more to a relationship than being faithful, Will. There's more to loving each other than duties and responsibilities. You can't see that because you don't want more from me. I'm not the woman for you. God, I wish I was but I'm not."

"I have given you everything I have. I don't know what more you want out of me. I don't want to walk away. I don't want any of this, and I damn sure don't want to be the man who makes you cry. Tell me what you want me to do, Bridget."

"I want you to go. I know it's a horrible thing to do, but I want it to be over. I can't do what you do. I can't live in the moment. I can't just be. I'm not wired like that." How was she going to watch him walk away? She stared straight ahead. She didn't have to look at him. She simply had to get through the next few moments and then she could cry.

"So I should walk away and not see you again?" He'd finally lost that reasonable tone and the question seemed wrenched from his throat.

She felt that he'd moved toward her, but she didn't think she could look at him and stay strong. "I'm sure we'll see each other, but we'll know what our relationship is so it won't hurt so much. I can move on."

Maybe in a couple of decades she would. Until then she would lock herself away and write about him.

It struck her suddenly that she really loved him. She wasn't going to murder him off in a book like she had the others. He hadn't done anything wrong. He'd been good to her. He simply couldn't love her. No. There would be no literary revenge waiting for him. She wanted him to be happy even if it was without her. He had so much to give.

He stepped around her and into the bedroom. Of course. His bag was in there. He would probably go and stay with Mitch for the night and then he would be gone, or maybe he would stay. Maybe he would take that vacation he needed so badly and find some other woman, one who wasn't too emotional, too damaged, too ill-tempered. He would find her and fall in love and be happy. She would be content if he could be happy. He deserved it. He deserved someone whose family wouldn't try to come after him. She had zero doubt that the next time her father needed something from her, he would hold the threat of ruining Will over her head again. He wouldn't hesitate and if he got bored, he'd do it for fun.

But once Will was gone, he would be safe and he could find what he deserved. It was the best gift she could give him.

"I need to talk to you." He seemed determined to make this harder than it had to be.

She shook her head, not turning to him because she could feel the tears slipping down her cheeks. "There's nothing to talk about."

"I have something to say."

Damn it. She'd thought he would be somewhat graceful. He was always polite, even in difficult situations, but it looked like he wasn't going to handle rejection well. Now he would tell her how stupid she was for dumping him, how she'd made a mistake and she would regret it. She would have to endure. She supposed he deserved his little revenge. It would even be good because then he wouldn't be so perfect. He would be another guy who put her down when she wasn't good enough for him. "Fine. Say what you have to say."

Arms came around her and suddenly she was surrounded by him, by his warmth, his scent, his strength. "Don't give up on me. Please, Bridget. I will figure this out. I'll find a way to give you what you need because I don't want to live without you. Please don't give up on me."

A sob threatened to tear from her chest. "I can't."

His arms tightened. "You can. You can tell me what's wrong. No matter how bad it is, I'll fix it."

She broke down. She could be strong by herself. She could force herself to stand tall, but with Will's arms around her, with his words in her ears, she couldn't help but break, and once the flood gates opened, she let loose. Tears—she hadn't known she'd had so many inside her—rushed out in great sobs. She wasn't sure when he turned her or if she'd done it, but she found herself chest to chest with him, his big arms holding her tight like he'd never let her go.

"It's okay, sweetheart. Go ahead. You cry all you like. I won't go anywhere. You understand me? You can't make me leave you."

She shook her head. "You need to."

His hand came up, cradling her neck. "No. I need to be here with you."

"I asked you to leave." Everyone else had left. Naturally the one man she wanted to leave wouldn't.

"And I'm sure it won't be the last time, and you should know that I won't. Not unless I am one-hundred-percent sure that it's in your best interest. I won't leave you. Even when you try to push me away. No one fights for you, do they?"

Her friends did, but it wasn't the same. Her family had always been

141

the fight. And she couldn't bring him into that world because no matter how hard she tried to distance, they always came back. She took a deep breath and forced herself to step away. Well, she tried. His arms were a cage, keeping her close. "Will, you have to leave. You can't stay."

He kissed her forehead. "Of course I can. I'm the Dom, remember."

"I'm not signing another stupid contract."

"Then we'll move on without one."

"You asshole. You have to leave."

"Give me one good reason."

She was going to have to lay it out for him. He was so stubborn. She needed to put it to him in the harshest terms possible. "Because I can't help my sister without hurting you. Because I'm resentful that my father can use you against me. I don't want to be vulnerable to him. So I'm kicking you out of my life. Do you understand?"

His gentle smile stumped her. "So much better than you can imagine."

She pushed away, and this time he let her have some distance. "What the hell is that supposed to mean?"

"It means I'm not stupid. I know what you look like when you're mad and you're not mad, Bridget. You're afraid. Your father dug up some crap on my past and he's threatened you with it. What's he planning on doing? Is he going to tell everyone my mother's a meth head and that I grew up dirt poor? Won't that shock the family?" He took a step toward her, his big body so reassuring she almost stepped back into his arms. "I don't care what your family thinks of me. They can all go to hell for what I care. You're the one who matters, and I know I can tell you anything and you'll be okay with it. As for your sister, I think she can take care of herself. Something's going on with her and Frankie. They're planning something. I don't know what."

She didn't really care what they were planning. What her father would do was all that mattered. "Okay, you don't care what my family thinks. I don't either. How about the hospital?"

He stopped for a moment and then nodded as though finally getting it. "Ah. So he threatened my job. Honey, I'm very good at my job. They're not going to fire me."

"My dad knows one of the board members. He's going to tell him about Sanctum and about what happened with Starr. He's going to tell them about your mom. He said no one would want a doctor with a history of addiction in his family."

Will actually laughed at that one. "Sweetheart, there would be no doctors then. Or very few. Unless I have a problem myself or I start writing prescriptions for my relatives, there's no issue. As for the BDSM stuff, they have no right to judge my sex life. If they do, Mitch will be happy to sue them and I would find a new job."

"He's going to ask his friends in the press to cover the Starr trial and make you look like an idiot."

He considered that for a moment. "Will you stand beside me?"

"Yes, but that's not the point."

"It is the point," Will said. "Let your father do his worst. Now let's go to bed. In the morning if you still want to go home, I'll make reservations. I would rather we stayed though. I think we can use the alone time. I found us a rental with a private pool. I'm going to keep you naked as much as possible."

She shook her head. "No. No. Will, I can't."

He pulled her close, and she didn't have the willpower to deny him. "You can. You can give me some time to sort this out. You can trust me to take care of you. If the worst happens, stay with me. I can handle a lot if you stay with me."

She dissolved again. It had almost been a relief to have it over. Now she was back with no hope of getting out with some tiny piece of her heart intact. "You deserve more."

He picked her up. God, did he know how good that felt? She suspected he knew how much she loved it when he picked her up and carried her around. "No. You deserve more, sweetheart. I'm going to figure it out. I promise. I'm going to figure out what you need."

"I need you to be safe."

He kissed her forehead as he started for the bedroom. "I'm safe. I'm good, Bridget. I want you to stop thinking for a minute. Just let us be tonight."

That was what he always wanted. He wanted to just be and she needed a future. But as he carried her to the bed, she knew she couldn't turn him away.

And when his body pressed hers into the soft comfort of the mattress, she finally stopped thinking and let herself feel, feel safe and cherished.

Even if it was only for the moment.

* * * *

Deep in the night, Will rolled cautiously out of bed. He dressed and as quietly as he could, he walked out into the living area of their suite.

It had been a close thing tonight. He'd almost lost her and he wasn't an idiot. That hadn't been all about her father. She was scared and sad. He'd done that to her.

He didn't know how to explain it to her. He was being stubborn and he'd put himself in a corner. She wouldn't believe him if he simply said the words. They didn't mean anything to him, but they seemed to mean the world to her. If he'd said them back to her at the beginning, they wouldn't be in this place.

He had to find a way to make her believe they could work because his whole soul rejected the idea of walking away from her. He was incapable of doing it. Somehow, this whole short-term affair that was supposed to get her out of his system had turned into something he needed to survive.

His tablet caught his eye. The hotel had Wi-Fi. Bridget's books were all over the Internet. His sister's words played through his head.

I was reading her before you started dating her. I love her stuff. She's funny and she has a lot to say about what a woman deserves. I guess really it's about what people deserve out of a relationship.

If he wanted to seduce Bridget into staying with him, maybe he should read what she considered romantic. She'd kind of written whole books about what she thought was sexy.

About what she wanted out of a relationship.

He picked up the tablet, downloaded the first book, and started to read.

When his cell trilled, he started. The world had been so quiet for hours, but now he could see the sun was starting to come up. He looked down at the number and his heart clenched a little.

Gatesville. His mom was using her weekly call.

He supposed it was almost noon back in Texas.

He didn't even think about letting it go. It was kismet. He didn't believe in a lot of spiritual crap, but he'd figured out a few things during the long night. He'd figured out that the only way to keep Bridget was to freaking love her, and the only way to do that was to let go of all the shit holding him back.

"Will you accept a call…"

"Yes, please."

There was a click and then his mother's voice came over the line. "William?"

She sounded surprised but then she probably was. He'd stopped taking her calls a long time ago. "Mother."

There was a little gasp. "It's really good to hear your voice." A sniffling sound came over the line. "Really good. How are you, son?"

"I'm not going to have some long discussion with you, Mother. I'm going to make you an offer and you can take or leave it. I will take your calls as long as you attend AA meetings and make a pledge to go to rehab when you get out. I will pay for the best rehab possible and the girls and I will come and visit you as long as you are sober and stay out of trouble."

"I've been sober for two years, Will." Her voice cracked. "I'm scared I won't be when I get out of here. I know you can't believe me but I want to stay clean."

He was surprised at the tears that sparked behind his eyes. "Then I'll help you."

There was a long pause. "Why? Why would you do that?"

"Because you're my mother. Because you brought me into this world and I think I'm finally grateful for that. I'm on vacation with my girlfriend, Mom, but I'll come down and see you when I get back and we'll talk."

They hung up a few minutes later, and it felt as though a massive weight had lifted off his shoulders. She might disappoint him again, but he'd done everything he could.

Would Bridget be proud of him?

Would Bridget believe him when he told her what he'd figured out some time in those long hours of the night?

He got to his feet, feeling more alive than he had in forever. A plan quickly formed in his head and he was eager to get started.

He would make her believe.

Chapter Eleven

Bridget sighed as she looked around the brunch gathering. All girls. No boys allowed so not a chance to get a glimpse of Will. Of course that seemed to be the way things were going today. When she'd gotten up he'd been nowhere to be found. He'd left a note that said he'd be back later and that was all.

Had he had a change of heart? She wouldn't blame him. It would be for the best. She wished he'd stuck around to tell her. He'd taken her to bed. He'd asked her not to give up on him, but somehow the night before had felt like good-bye.

"Hey, grumpy." Serena slid into the chair beside her. "You look like you're going to a funeral and not a wedding. Have a Bellini."

She didn't feel like drinking. She figured she needed to be sober to go the next round with Will. At some point he would show up. He wouldn't leave no matter how difficult she'd been. He'd still be kind to her even as he was leaving. "I'll pass. Sorry about the grumpy. I didn't sleep well last night."

Serena grinned. "Did Will keep you up? I have to say, I was nervous about the two of you getting together. He seemed distant and that's not what you need."

Maybe he'd seemed that way in the beginning, but from the moment she'd said yes to him, there hadn't been a lot of space between them. "He isn't distant. Not most of the time. Most of the time he's on top of me."

Serena laughed, her eyes lighting up. "I know. Isn't that great? You two look good together. Sometimes it takes the right woman to bring a man out of his shell. That man used to be cold. I believe in all the time he's been at Sanctum he's said two words to me, and then he starts dating you and he's always opening doors for me when my guys aren't around. The poor man carried all my crap up to my room yesterday. Tristan was being a wiggle worm and I couldn't handle the bag, my purse, and my laptop bag. But no problem. Super Doc to the rescue. Then he came in and took a look at Tristan for me because he was running a slight fever and I was nervous. Apparently Tristan's starting to teethe. Will told me to let him chew on something cold and he stopped crying. He still remembers his rotation in Peds."

"He's a nice guy." He was a nice guy and she was a woman with a bad attitude. Could they have lasted longer if she hadn't brought him here where her family problems seemed to have pushed her over the edge?

Serena sat back, regarding her. "I don't think you understand what I'm saying. He hasn't been that nice. Oh, according to club gossip, he's really good in bed, but he never spends a whole night with any of his lovers and he's usually done with them after one go. He's never rude but always cold. He takes the D/s very seriously. It's why I was worried. I thought you would have a problem with an über Dom."

He liked to spank her, but that was just play. "Will? He's not a super Dom. He never truly tops me except in the bedroom. He's the kind of guy who gently suggests. He wanted me to stop working at night. How crazy is that? He seems to think that I need down time. So he started rubbing my feet, but only if I wasn't typing. Does that sound like an über Dom?"

"How often have you worked at night in the last two weeks?" Serena asked the question with a sly grin on her face.

"I…" Holy shit. She'd stopped. She sat with him now. He didn't even have to rub her feet anymore. She set the computer aside when he came home. "I don't. Damn him. He trained it out of me."

Serena nodded. "Sneaky Dom. He's totally changed his approach because he figured out what you need. Most Doms aren't so adaptable. I thought it was going to be a train wreck, but he totally loves you."

That was where she was wrong. "He doesn't. He's made that very plain."

"He said he doesn't love you? Or he hasn't said anything yet? It's early. Guys can be dumb."

"And so can I. I said the words. He very gently explained that he couldn't return them."

"Are you kidding me? He said he couldn't love you?" Serena's face took on that expression she got whenever her loved ones where threatened. Bridget liked to think of it as her "Momma Bear" expression. She needed to shut that shit down or Serena would be cornering poor Will.

"He told me he doesn't believe in the word, and you know what that means. It's okay. It's not going to work long term. I didn't go into this expecting to find the love of my life." That was the way it had worked out though.

Serena relaxed. "Oh, good. He's just stupid then."

"He's not stupid," Bridget shot back. "He's one of the smartest men I've ever met. Hello, brain surgeon. He's just…I don't know. He needs someone different."

Serena groaned. "Get your self-esteem in check, Eeyore, because I'm calling bullshit. I've seen how he looks at you and how's he's changed his whole life for you. If he's saying he doesn't believe in love it's because he's a dumbass, and you can't hold that against him. It would be really mean to dump him because he's emotionally stupid."

"Serena, you don't understand."

"I am married to Jacob Dean. Trust me. I understand emotionally stupid men. Now, I am also married to my gorgeous drama king, Adam, so it all…I was going to say it all works out but it's more like grand and beautiful chaos. And that's kind of what love is really. Trust me. I've been watching him with you." Her hand slid over Bridget's with a comforting squeeze. "You took care of me for years. I want you happy. Don't let a single word screw things up. What you call love, he might call devotion."

Bridget shook her head. "Teamwork. He called it good teamwork."

Serena gasped and seemed to share in Bridget's disdain. "Oh, that is horrible. I'll have Adam work on him. The man does know how to use his words. Luckily, Jake knows how to use his tongue for different things. In some men's cases, sex is how they communicate. It's the only way they know how."

He'd asked her not to give up on him. She'd thrown a shit storm at him the night before and he'd asked her not to give up on him.

What was she willing to throw away over a single word? Over the possibility of failure?

"Bridge, are you okay?" Serena asked. "I've never seen you cry before."

She'd never let anyone see her cry before. It had been a weakness, something to hide. That was before Will. He was right. No one ever fought for her. Will had fought for her the night before—he'd been forced to fight her. Any other man would have walked out the door, not fought to stay and held her all night.

What was a word worth in the face of his care and devotion?

She stood up, jostling the table. All around her, family members stared up as though they'd been waiting for her to cause trouble. They started to talk behind their hands.

Amy left the group she'd been talking to and made her way to Bridget, a concerned look on her face. "Hey, you okay?"

She was about as far from okay as a woman could get, but it was her sister's wedding day and she didn't want to drag Amy into her drama. She would have enough of her own. "I have to go."

Amy put a hand on her elbow. "Uhm, I think you should stay."

"I have to find Will." She couldn't leave things the way they were. She needed to find a way to make the idiocy of the previous night go away. She would sit down with Will and do what she should have done in the first place. She would talk to him and make a plan about how to deal with her father.

Amy looked over her shoulder and a smile lit up her face. "Oh, I think he's going to be around. Sit down, Bridget."

"Holy hot doc." Serena grinned. "Damn, that man is fine. Don't tell my men I said that. They can be sensitive."

There was a hum of excitement all around her, and when she turned, it was easy to see why. Will was striding into the room wearing nothing but his leathers and boots. He was heartstoppingly gorgeous and he was carrying what looked like a mountain of flowers her way.

Every eye in the room was on him and every woman in the room was talking about him.

"Did Amy hire a stripper?"

"Oh, I know who I'm doing this weekend."

"We need to figure out how much Bridget paid him and offer him more."

Will stopped right in front of her and turned to her cousin Violet, who had spoken that last bit of wisdom. His eyes narrowed and his jaw took the consistency of granite as he stared down Violet, who flinched. "There isn't enough money in the world to get me to touch you. You offend me." His whole face softened as he turned back to Bridget. "Now you, on the other hand, you make me happy." He gave her a wink before turning to Amy and passing her one of the two large bouquets he was carrying. "For the beautiful bride." He then passed the second one to Serena. "And to my fiancée's very sweet best friend. Ladies, this is my apology for kidnapping the maid of honor. I promise she will make the wedding, but don't expect her to be able to walk down the aisle properly because I am going to fuck her until she can't move."

Bridget felt her jaw drop open before she mustered the necessary strength to yell at him. "Will!"

His lips curled up in the sexiest grin she'd ever seen. "Hey, I know you prize honesty, sweetheart. And I prize something else." He reached for her hands.

She let him because she was still reeling over the fact that he was here and he was dressed like a sub's wettest dream and he'd told off her awfulest cousin. "Will, I know we need to talk, but…"

And that was when he cuffed her. One minute he was sweetly holding her hands, and the next he was slapping a pair of handcuffs on her. They were metal, but lined with super soft material that kept the cold off her wrists.

Serena smiled approvingly. "Oh, I know that brand well. Such fun."

Amy's mouth had dropped open and she stared at the cuffs. "Is he going to arrest her? Why did he…"

"Amy, your sister and I are involved in a D/s relationship. I will leave the explanation of that to the expert." He nodded to Serena before tugging on the cuffs and pulling Bridget out of her chair.

She stood on suddenly shaky legs. What was he doing? "Will, you can't handcuff me in front of the bridal party."

"Oh, but sweetheart, I just did. I think everyone will agree that I can. They'll agree I can do this, too." He leaned over and gently shoved his shoulder into her midsection, catching her in a fireman's hold and easily lifting her.

"You did that very well, Will," Serena agreed. "And thank you for the flowers. They're gorgeous. I'll make sure to perform her duties until she can."

"Bridget, are you sure this is all right?" Amy asked.

Bridget tried to bring her head up so she could see her sister. It wasn't easy. She caught a glimpse of Amy's lovely Jimmy Choos. How did one explain BDSM to a woman who thought marrying a gay guy was the key to her happiness? "It's only play. He would never hurt me. Embarrass me, but never hurt me."

Serena took over. "Come on, hon. I'm going to give you some new reading material. Have you really never read your sister's books?"

"I haven't had a lot of reading time," Amy replied.

Story of her life. Everyone had an opinion of her books but very few had read them. "Will, put me down and we'll talk about this like adults."

She heard the loud smack before she felt it. Will turned and started for the door. "Nope. We're going to do this my way. I'm going to talk and you're going to listen, and if you don't, I have a very nice ball gag all prepped and prepared back in our room. Good morning, Mrs. Slaten."

Shit. She twisted her head and saw her mother walking into the room still wearing her big-ass Chanel sunglasses and carrying a Bloody Mary.

"Good morning, young man. Bridget. That skirt makes your backside look smaller. Very nice." She tottered off toward the tables. That was her mom. Seeing her being carried away in handcuffs and all she could comment about was how her backside didn't look as hideous as usual.

Will kept moving. "Did you like the flowers? Did they seem at all familiar?"

She was staring at his ungodly gorgeous backside. "Will, I don't care about the flowers. We need to talk." But there was something familiar about the flowers. "I think I wrote a scene like that."

He turned down the hall toward the elevators. "You did indeed. In *Love Wickedly*, the youngest of the Coleman brothers takes flowers to the heroine's mom and sister to apologize for kidnapping her from Sunday dinner."

He'd read her book? It had been her first book, and it involved three brothers and one very lucky woman. A woman she admitted had a lot of Bridget in her. "So you thought you would play out a fantasy? You didn't have to go this far."

"Oh, but I do." He stopped at the elevator and pressed the button, paying absolutely no attention to the people around them. "I'm going to prove something to you. There were three brothers in that book. They each had one obvious personality trait. There was the sweet one who took care of her and made sure she had everything she needed. There was the smart one who always knew what to say. And then there was the Dom, and he knew how to give her what she needed in the bedroom. I think my sister is right, and if you put all three of those men together, you get Bridget's perfect man. Guess what, sweetheart? I'm going to prove to you that I'm that man."

The elevator doors opened and Will entered. Bridget tried to look up before he turned. She noticed everyone else had decided to take another car.

"Will, you don't have to prove anything. Seriously, I was wrong to push you." Serena's words had gotten to her. It was important that she stopped only thinking about her needs and gave a little back to him. "It's okay. I don't want you to leave. God, I'll be miserable if you leave me. If you want me to sign another contract, I will. I know you need that to feel safe."

She felt him shift and suddenly her feet were on the floor, his arms balancing her. He stared at her for a moment while the elevator made its progress. "I only need you to feel safe. I had a talk with Frankie last night. You know, he's not a bad guy and I think your sister knows what she's getting into. But that talk got me thinking. Then after you went to sleep, I read your book. Only the first one, but I'm going to read them all. I get it. Love isn't just a word. It's the most important word but we have to define it for ourselves. We can't let someone else own what love means to us. I've been using a definition straight out of my childhood, but I need to figure out how to define that word as a man, not a boy. Tell me what it means when you say you love me."

She didn't even think about prevaricating. She told him exactly what she thought. "It means I'll never leave you. It means I need you to be happy more than I need to be happy. It means that when I'm with you, I finally feel like myself. It's like I was always looking for this piece of me and it turns out you had it with you all along."

He brushed back her hair. "I love you, Bridget."

Tears threatened again. Damn this man. She'd cried more since she met him than all the years before, but she had to admit it felt good. It felt good to not have to hide. Still, it was hard to understand how he'd gone from not being able to say the word to giving it to her with such conviction.

The door opened and he lifted her up again, this time cradling her in his arms.

"You don't have to say those words, Will. I'm good. I promise I'm not going to throw another fit and try to kick you out. I'll sign the contract."

He made quick work of the distance between the elevator and their suite and settled her on her feet again. He opened the door and then pulled her inside by the cuffs. "You will sign a contract, but not the one you're thinking of. And you didn't throw a fit. You were scared. Your dad scared you, but I'm going to take care of that, too. I'm going to protect you and make sure he doesn't have any power over us again."

Her eyes widened as she took in the changes he'd made to the living area of their suite. A buffet table had been set up, and Will had laid out a wide array of toys. There was a flogger, a crop, two vibes, a butt plug. Holy shit, was that a violet wand? "What did you do?"

"I renovated. It's okay. The room is billed to your dad. He's going to get charged for what I did to the ceiling."

She looked up. There was now a very sturdy hook and chain attached to the ceiling.

He grinned at her and led her over to the place where the chain dangled. "Don't worry about it. Taggart and Dean helped me. I assure you they know what they're doing. And the cuffs were made for bondage so they won't hurt your wrists." He looped the chain around her cuffs and she suddenly found herself bound to the hook. "See, that's perfect."

"Will, this isn't a dungeon." But it felt like one. With her hands bound above her, she felt vulnerable and open to him. Despite her misgivings, her body was definitely heating up in all the right places. "The maids could come in at any time."

"Nope. I slipped the *Do Not Disturb* sign on the door. We're all alone and I want you to ask me."

"Ask you when you went insane?" She was fascinated by the change in him. He was more relaxed than she'd ever seen him, as if he'd come to some inner decision and now he was at peace.

He picked up the crop and slapped it against his hand. He turned and studied her, his eyes predatory. "I went insane the moment I saw you, and I don't want to go back. Now are you going to be a bratty girl who gets a spanking? Or the sweet sub who gets all the treats?"

It was far hotter in the room than she'd suspected at first. "Will, you can't make all our problems go away with a flick of the crop."

She knew she'd made a mistake the minute she saw that tiny shake of his head. And then he moved to the side and she nearly screamed when she felt that crop come down hard on her ass. Once and then again and again until she'd counted five. The pain flared, roaring through her system and then settling down to a pleasant warmth as his hand cupped her curves through the filmy material of her skirt.

"So you want to be the brat?" He moved to her front, setting the crop back down before turning around to face her. He moved into her space, his hands starting at her breasts and skimming their way down to the waistband of her skirt. "That was a little taste of what I have planned for you. Let's see how you like the crop against your naked skin."

He eased the skirt down, over her hips and thighs until he pulled it off and she was left standing in her wedge sandals and the embroidered tank top she'd picked out because Will told her it made her breasts look good. She'd known she was dressing for him, hoping to smooth things over this morning. She hadn't quite planned on things going this way.

The crop came down again on the fleshy part of her ass. She whimpered but had to admit the man knew how to wield a crop. Her body was warming up, her muscles heating and preparing for what would come.

"I can be good." If he wanted to play, she could play. She still wasn't sure exactly what was going on, but she suspected this wasn't his revenge on her for trying to throw him out. He wasn't that man. If he told her he wanted to try, then he wanted to try.

He took her not exactly cheap tank and tore it right down the middle, sending sequins and rhinestones clattering to the floor. His hands went straight for her breasts, thumbs rasping over hardened nipples. "Ask me."

She couldn't think about anything but his hands on her body. "Ask you?"

"About love." He leaned over and licked one nipple. Her whole body started to quiver. "I've heard your definition. Now you need to hear mine."

If he said teamwork, she was going to smile and agree with him. Anything to keep him touching her. Anything to keep him with her. Serena was right. She couldn't give this man up over the definition of a word. "What do you mean when you say I love you?"

"I mean I want you. I mean I can't breathe without you. I mean you invade my every thought, and my whole fucking world lights up when you walk into a room."

Oh, that was better than teamwork. "I want to touch you, Will. I want to hold you."

He brought his head off her breast and loomed over her. "I want that, too, but only after I make a few things clear. When I say I love you, I mean you're my safe place, and don't think I take that lightly. Don't think it will always be easy sailing. I'm going to start visiting my mother to make an attempt at salvaging some sort of relationship with her. I'd like to save her if I can. I didn't before. No child can save a parent. They can merely survive, but I'm an adult now and for all she did, I think I would regret not trying. I want you to go with me."

Yep. She was crying again. "I would love to. I want to help you, babe. I'll help any way I can." Her heart swelled at the thought of him reaching out to her and trusting her with something so personal. She wouldn't let him down. A terrible thought struck her, and she had to hope this newfound openness and forgiveness didn't go too far. "Please don't tell me you think I should try to reconcile with my dad."

He stepped away. "No. What my mother did was selfish, but when I look back, I can see she was never malicious. She got caught in a bad cycle. Your father is simply an atrocious human being. I told you. I'm going to take care of your father. When I say I love you, I mean I'll protect you. You don't need walls around me. You don't need walls anymore because I'll take care of you. I think I understand what you need now. Tell me, was I right about the characters?"

His voice had gone deep again, his hands on her body. He stroked her as he waited for a reply.

She sighed as his fingers skimmed down her belly and over her pussy. There was no way to hide it. From the moment he'd touched her, she'd been wet and ready for him. She'd never responded to a man like that before and she knew she never would again. Will was hers. And he was right. "I took what I wanted in my dream man and made him into three brothers. It's only a fantasy, Will. I fear what real ménage would be like with all the laundry and three men demanding I listen to their work stories. Hopefully they all have jobs. Then they would probably fight over the TV and I would never get to watch *The Bachelor*."

He reached up and gave her nipple a nice twist. "Stay with me, sweetheart. So let me get this straight. Your dream man is thoughtful."

Like he'd been thoughtful. She couldn't help but smile at him. "Yes. He's thoughtful. He's the kind of man who gently maneuvers me into relaxing more."

His hand was on her pussy, lightly playing, making her crazy. "So you caught that. Well, I'll have to be sneakier next time. Bridget, I promise to always think of you, to put your needs before mine."

He stepped away.

"Hey, already breaking your promise here," she complained. "Because I am definitely feeling needy."

He was standing at the table, and when he turned back, he held a set of nipple clamps in his hands. "I fully intend to take care of all your needs, to make you understand that you don't need three men. The only one you need is right here."

He dropped to his knees and sucked her nipple into his mouth, tonguing her and making her writhe. He wasn't playing around. It seemed he meant business. He nipped at her breast, and when she thought she couldn't take it anymore, he leaned back and slipped the clamp on.

"Oh, god." The alligator clamp bit into her flesh, sending the sensation through her system.

He went to work on the opposite breast, preparing it. When both nipples were well clamped, a thin chain running between them, he stood and admired his work. He played lightly with the chain, sending delicious heat through her body. "Don't you look pretty like this? So the middle brother is the smart one. He's the one who always knows what to say. He's the clever one who would think up inventive ways to make the heroine go crazy."

The clamps were already doing that for her. They were making her restless, and somehow those damn things seemed to have a direct line to her pussy. "You don't need to do this. I know you're smart. You're the smartest man I know."

He was back at his mad buffet of torture implements, selecting one of the larger plugs. "Oh, sweetheart, I have been very stupid when it comes to you." He took his time, lubing up the really big plug from its rounded tip down to right above the flared base that would help ensure that sucker stayed where he put it. "I haven't always said the right things but I'm going to start." He turned and faced her, plug in hand. "I love you, Bridget."

She had to laugh because apparently when Will said he loved her he meant she should take his large plug up her ass. When she thought about it, it was a fitting way to prove her love. "You're going to fill me up, aren't you, Doctor?"

His leathers suddenly looked way too small. His cock was tenting them nicely. "I like that. I see we're going to have some very kinky medical exams in your future. But tonight I'm going to make sure you feel me everywhere. And I'm definitely going to say all the right things." He disappeared behind her. "This is the most gorgeous ass I've ever seen in my life."

She'd always thought it was too big, but she could become grateful for it if Will kept telling her how pretty it was. "What are you going to do to me, Doc?"

She knew what he was going to do, but she loved to hear him talk dirty. She trembled when she felt him move in behind her.

"Spread your legs for me. I know it's hard, but you look so gorgeous when you're submitting to my every disgusting desire. Do you know how much I like to fuck your ass? Do you know how good it feels when that pretty hole is wrapped around my dick? Do you know how good I feel when you're wrapped around me? When you hold me and all I can see and smell and touch is you—that's my whole world."

Oh, he was so stinking good at saying the right things. She managed to give him what he wanted. Very carefully, she spread her legs and opened herself to him. Almost immediately she felt the cool tip of the plug against her asshole. Every breath made the clamps move, and now she felt the sweet pressure of the plug working in.

He fucked her with the plug, moving in and out of her body with an easy rhythm that made her want to scream. "I'm not going back to my condo, Bridget. I'm moving in with you because wherever you are, that's where my home is. I don't want to spend a minute apart from you that I don't have to."

She groaned as he slid the plug home, nestling it deep inside. She could feel the flat base of the plug fitted between her cheeks. "I think we should get a house. Serena's neighborhood is nice."

He was smiling when he moved around to face her. "Then a house you shall have, sweetheart. But there's one more brother, isn't there?"

She shivered at the thought. She'd written that character from her darkest fantasies. She'd wanted a lover who was sensitive and smart but oh, how she'd wanted one who could dominate her, too. "The oldest Coleman brother was the Dom."

He reached up and tugged on the chain between her breasts, setting her nipples on fire. "That's the part I love to play and that's the part you won't forget. I'll lightly and sneakily top you in our real life. Don't think I won't. I'll suggest and make the way easy for you, but that all changes the minute we enter the bedroom, and by bedroom I mean any room I'm going to fuck you in. Who's in charge of this, Bridget?"

There was only one answer to that question. "You are."

"I'll want you naked. I'll want you on your knees. I'll demand that you take my cock every way possible. In your mouth and between your breasts. In your ass and definitely in your sweet cunt. All of those things belong to me." He flicked a nipple, making her jump. "This body is mine." He put his hand against her breast. "Tell me this heart is mine, too."

What the hell had she done to get him? "Everything I have is yours. Unfortunately, you get my bratty mouth, too."

He leaned over and kissed her, his mouth devouring hers. "I love your bratty mouth. It gives me the chance to spank you and torture you. You never bore me and you've made me understand that I need a partner, not a responsibility. You're my partner, Bridget. I can count on you. You have no idea how much I needed that."

"I need you, too. I love my friends and they've been a godsend, but I've been waiting for you, Will. I love you so much."

His fingers went to the ties on his leathers, freeing his cock with a few twists. Long and thick, his dick pointed her way and she couldn't take her eyes off it. He stroked himself with that big hand of his. "Then take me. Take all of me. Know that you don't need any other man than me."

He spread her legs even further, his hands bracing her, and she felt his cock start to penetrate. With one long thrust, he took her pussy, diving deep inside her cunt to connect them. He held her up, balancing her and making her feel secure.

"Do you know how good it feels to be inside you?" His mouth hovered over hers.

She was held up only by his strong arms and the hook he'd planted in the ceiling. It should have scared her. At the very least it should have made her uncomfortable, and yet she'd never felt safer. She didn't need defenses against him. He was the one place in the world where she could let go and be exactly who she was. She squeezed him tight, loving the groan that elicited from him. "I know how good it is to have your cock inside me. What are you waiting for?"

He slowly pulled out. "I like this position. You're so fucking tight. I won't last long so I need to make this good for you." He pressed back in. His hands tightened on her hips so he could grind against her clit. "I like you like this. My sweet sub."

Always his. "My gorgeous Master."

"You know that's true. Yours, Bridget. Don't you ever forget it." His face took on the hard lines of a man on a mission and he stroked into her again and again. He picked up the pace and her whole body came to vivid life.

There was nothing for her to do but feel. He'd put his mark on her, tied her hands, made it so all she could do was take what he gave her. Trust. He wanted her trust and she gave it to him. She'd never trusted a man, loved a man the way she did Will Daley.

His cock rammed deep, almost immediately hitting her G-spot. All she could do was moan and let that pleasure shiver through her body. She could feel him everywhere. He was there in the way her breasts jangled in the clamps, in the pressure of the plug in her ass. His hand moved to help keep the plug deep inside. He was there kissing her mouth and fucking her in the sweetest way possible.

And his words started to penetrate. "I love you, Bridget. I love you so fucking much."

She let the orgasm take her, riding that wave of pure pleasure until she couldn't think about anything but him.

He stiffened and she felt the wash of his come inside her. It filled her and made her warm.

He slipped out, a wicked grin on his face. "Now we get to the fun stuff. I've been dying to use that violet wand on you."

Nope. She didn't need any other men. She got the feeling she would barely be able to handle the one she had.

Chapter Twelve

Bridget stood next to Will and looked at her sister and Frankie. They were stunning in their wedding finery. Amy was wearing an impossibly gorgeous Vera Wang sheath with a diamond tiara instead of a veil. Frankie was stylish in his Gucci tux. She had to sigh because they really were the most beautiful couple she'd ever seen. And guilt sat in her gut. She hadn't talked to her sister. She'd chosen Will. In the end, it had to be that way. Will was the love of her life. She owed him everything, but she couldn't stand the fact that she'd betrayed her sister.

"It's going to be all right, sweetheart." Will had been mysterious all afternoon. He was planning something. He'd been on the phone a couple of times, but when she would ask, he shrugged her off.

"I hope so." She waved as her sister walked over. Her baby sister. God, she remembered when Amy couldn't tie her own shoes and now she was a gorgeous woman.

"Are you sure you're okay?" The deed was done. They'd been married on the beach not thirty minutes earlier, but Bridget had to ask the question.

A secret smile lit Amy's lips. "I'll let you know in a day or two, but I think everything's going to work out fine."

Shit. Her sister thought once she slept with Frankie, everything would be okay. "Amy, I have to talk to you."

Will's hand tightened on her. "You can talk after the reception."

Amy laughed. "Oh, I was wondering when you were going to do the big sister talk."

"There's a big sister talk?" Frankie was suddenly at his bride's side. He slid an arm around Amy's waist. "I would love to hear this. You look stunning in that tiara, love. Didn't I tell you how lovely it would look?"

"You just want to put it on James later," Amy teased.

"Who's James?" Bridget got the sudden feeling she wasn't sure she wanted to know.

"I can bet," Will said out of the side of his mouth.

Bridget threw him a dirty look. She might be his sub in the bedroom, but she still had a say out here in the real world.

Amy leaned over. "His lover, Bridge. He's far too young for Frankie, but he won't listen to me. He's all about the twink, if you know what I mean."

Bridget frowned at her sister and pointed her finger. She couldn't do it as well as Serena since she didn't have the mom thing yet, but she put all her righteous indignation into that point anyway. "You know."

"Of course I know. I've known all along," Amy replied, leaning into Frankie.

Frankie frowned. "I'm going to have to work on passing for straight. What gives me away?"

"Well, it didn't help that you practically devoured my bestie with your eyes," Bridget admitted.

"Ah, the lovely Chris." Frankie winked flirtatiously. "Now there's a mature man I might be able to get into."

"He has a boyfriend."

Frankie shrugged. "He might not always have one. If he finds himself alone, give me a call and I'll comfort him. James and I are only casual dates, though I will probably make him wear that tiara tonight. He'll look cute in it. A little prince. I'm not wasting my wedding night."

"Will someone tell me what's going on here?" She was confused. Someone had definitely left her out of the joke.

"Let's just say Frankie and I have a lot in common. We both have horrible fathers who don't accept us for who we are," Amy explained.

Frankie nodded. "I was told to get married—to a woman, of course—or I would be disinherited."

"And you know Father wants to merge with Frankie's father's company before he sells out and screws everyone over." A stubborn light hit Amy's eyes.

"You knew." Oh thank god. "I couldn't tell you."

Frankie's arm tightened around Amy's shoulders as though comforting her. "Because of Will. Well, we knew there was a reason your father had been looking into him. It explains the conversation I had with Will earlier."

Will gave Amy an enigmatic smile. "You're sure you're all right with what's about to happen?"

"I'm great. We looked at our numbers. We're good," Amy assured him.

"Numbers? What numbers?" Bridget was about to scream if someone didn't tell her what was going on.

Amy reached out and gave her a huge hug, squeezing her tight. "Don't worry anymore, Bridget. I'm going to follow in your footsteps and blaze my own trail. I've spent too much time being the good girl because I was afraid to fight back. You taught me how."

"Fight back?" Her stomach turned. "You can't do that. Amy, you know he won't fight fair. He'll destroy you."

Amy stepped back and took Frankie's hand again. "Not if we destroy him first. And your man there, I like him. He doesn't fight fair either. Tell Mr. Taggart we're ready for the media portion of the evening and that I sincerely hope he chooses to stay on at Slaten Industries. After all, we're thinking of relocating our corporate offices in the near future. He tells me Dallas is nice this time of year. And I'll go and let Mitchell know we'll need his services in about an hour."

She watched as her sister and Frankie walked away hand in hand toward the center of the elegantly decorated reception hall. "What the hell is going on, Will? And it's summer. Ian lies. Dallas is a stinking hellhole this time of the year. Relocating? My father will never relocate."

Amy needed Mitchell. Why would Amy need a lawyer? Slaten Industries had a ton of lawyers. A whole stinking department of them, so why would her sister use Ian Taggart's lawyer?

Why would her sister marry a man who didn't want to sleep with her?

"Frankie has a seat on the board now, doesn't he?" A seat on the board meant he had a vote. Bridget quickly ran down the board in her head. There was more than a quorum right here at the wedding.

Why would her sister consult an outside lawyer? Because she didn't want their father to know she was going to try to take him down.

Will smiled at her. "Have I ever told you how smart you are?"

"Actually no."

"Sorry, sweetheart. That's an oversight. I was far too busy looking at your boobs." He grabbed her hand and started to lead her toward the back of the room where the AV equipment and the DJ were set up. "You are brilliant though. I really do love your mind, too."

She looked ahead and saw the McKay-Taggart contingent standing beside the projector. Her sister had put together some sort of media show for the reception. It was supposed to be a montage of her and Frankie's lives. She was sure it was lovely and would bring a tear to her eye, but she still had questions.

"Why does Amy think the board will vote her way? If she doesn't pull this off, my father will destroy her." It was a gutsy move. It was spectacular, but it could also prove fatal if she didn't pull it off.

"Ah, you figured it out, did you?" Ian Taggart looked surprisingly happy. He was usually a dour man who frowned a lot. He was good at frowning, but his lips were turned up in a brilliant smile and he had his big hand on his wife's slightly rounded belly, holding her close to his body. "This is one of those moves where if you don't kill your prey, he comes back to take you out."

"That would be my point entirely," she shot back. "We need to make sure it's going to work before she tries it."

Adam was behind the projector, working the computer attached to it. "It's going to work. Trust me, after I run this footage, all hell's going to break loose. And it's all thanks to Will there."

Charlotte Taggart laid her hand over Ian's, both resting on the baby in her belly. "Thank you, Will. He's been so crabby. This has made him happier than you can imagine."

Chris and Jeremy were standing off to the side with Serena and Jake, but it was easy to tell they were talking about what was going on, too. Everyone knew except her.

"What have you done, Will?"

"Consider it a wedding present," Will said.

"To my sister?"

He pulled her close and lowered his forehead to hers. "No. To you. You are going to marry me, right? I remember you promising to sign any contract I wanted."

Her heart threatened to stop, and she couldn't help but put her hands on that face she'd grown to love. "Are you serious?"

"Marry me. I know it's quick, but…"

Hey, she never argued with her Master. Much. "Yes."

He lifted her up, his mouth meeting hers. "I love you."

She loved hearing those words from him. "I love you, too. Now tell me what my present is."

He set her on her feet. "I'd rather show you. I didn't actually find this. Ian did, but technically he worked for your father so he couldn't use it. However, I hired him and then talked to Amy and Frankie, who agreed this is the perfect time to premiere this film." He turned to Adam. "I think now's as good as any. Mitch, Amy wants to make sure you're ready to stand as a witness to the board meeting."

Mitch had been quiet for the whole wedding, but Bridget hadn't missed how his eyes every so often slid to find Laurel. Mitch nodded. "I am indeed. I've foregone alcohol all stinking day so I can make sure everything is done by the company bylaws. He won't legally find a way around it."

Laurel stood beside him, a laptop bag on her shoulder. "I'm ready to take the minutes. And then someone get Mr. Grumpy a Scotch."

Holy shit. This was really happening.

The lights dimmed and suddenly there was a show playing on the screen over the bride's table. All of Bridget's relatives turned, obviously ready to see some sweet film about the bride and groom.

Bridget gasped. Yeah, that wasn't the bride and groom. The film showed what looked to be an empty hotel room. "What's happening?"

"Magic," Ian Taggart replied.

Will leaned over and whispered in her ear. "Taggart found out that your father keeps a standing date at this hotel every week. He makes it a point to find out all the bad shit about a client before it bites him or the client in the ass, so he had Liam O'Donnell and Li's new partner bug the hotel. He thought he'd find your dad with his mistress."

"He always has a couple. That won't change things. Everyone knows." Her mother couldn't care less.

"Honey, would you say your family is very accepting of alternative lifestyles?"

"God, no." Her eyes widened as she saw her father and his friend enter the room. The woman on the screen was lovely. A sequined dress adorned her curvy body and she had to be forty years younger than her perverted old-dude dad.

"What is the meaning of this?" Her father had stood up and was glaring at the back of the room.

On screen, he sat down on the bed, his back to the camera, which was good because she didn't want to see her father's junk if he took his pants off. The pretty hooker stood in front of him and started to undress.

"Turn it off now. Right fucking now or I'll have your head, Taggart!" Her dad was stumbling as he tried to run through the tightly packed tables and chairs.

Taggart flipped him off. "I quit."

There was a gasp that went through the crowd. It drew Bridget's attention back to the screen where the hooker was doing a striptease. She had pretty breasts and a lovely face.

And a penis.

Her heart nearly stopped and tears of great joy threatened. "Is that my father with a pre-op tranny hooker? Please tell me that's my father with a pre-op tranny hooker. It will make up for all the shitty Christmases."

Her dad had stopped, staring at the screen as though he thought it was all a dream and he could force himself to wake up.

Taggart stepped up next to her, patting her shoulder. "See, it's always the blowhard righteous assholes who end up getting busted with a hooker. I told you it was magic. That right there, that's a gift. A gift to me. Damn, I feel good."

The shouting had already started, and she could see her father had come out of his stupor and was pushing his way through the shocked crowd. He was screaming, his face florid. "I will see you never work a day in your life, Taggart."

"That would be great. I could use a vacation," Taggart replied.

Her father stared at her and then pointed a finger her way. "You did this."

Will moved in front of her. "No. I did. And if you ever try to come near her again, you'll deal with me, and no amount of money will save you. I won't fight fair and you won't see me coming. Are we understood?"

Taggart was grinning as though this was the best show ever. "You know we could settle this the fight club way."

"I said no fight club!" Charlotte Taggart yelled and her husband shrugged.

"She never lets me have fun. And Slaten, if you come after Bridget, you'll find out why I was a Green Beret because I'll have Will's back. We all will." He gave her a nod and stepped back.

Her father turned a lovely shade of purple and stormed out.

Bridget just shook her head. They'd done it. They'd taken the old man down. Will had done it for her.

Amy seemed perfectly calm as she took the microphone.

"Good evening, everyone. I deeply apologize for tonight's entertainment. We seem to have gotten off track. I think this would be a perfect time to call a meeting of the board of Slaten Industries. As you all know, my loving father placed a morality code on all board members, stating that any one of you could lose all stock and place in the company if the majority found you guilty of loose morals. We have a quorum here and my personal lawyer is ready to witness the meeting. If you'll all follow me." She was polished and cool as Frankie led her down the steps.

Will hugged her tight. "She's going to help Frankie take over his father's company next week. They made a deal. They're getting divorced in six months, but I doubt they'll ever go their separate ways. Those two really do love each other."

For a man who hadn't believed in the word, he threw it out often now. And he'd helped do this for her. "This is the best day of my life, Will Daley."

"Back at you, sweetheart," he replied. "But let's see if I can top it next week."

* * * *

Will looked at his gorgeous girl as she stood by the ocean. The breeze gently blew her hair back. She was dressed in a lovely white sarong, but he had to admit he was looking forward to seeing her in nothing at all.

"You look like a satisfied man." Mitch stepped up next to him, a beer in his hand.

"I'm a married man." As of two hours ago, Bridget was officially Bridget Daley. His wife. It had taken a few days to settle the formalities and to get his sisters over to the islands, but they'd come and his friends had stayed. It hadn't been as grand as Amy and Frankie's, but it was going to last. He was going to love that girl for the rest of his life.

"Good." Mitch nodded. "And I don't want you to worry about Laurel. I promise I don't have designs on her."

He'd softened up on that. Bridget and Laurel had started the process and then Lila and Lisa had completed it. Laurel was a smart woman. Mitch was a good man. "Treat her right or you'll answer to me."

Mitch's face went a perfect blank. "I'm going to treat her like any employee. I have no intention of touching her. She's off limits. She couldn't…she's so young. Hell, she would run away screaming if she figured out what I wanted from a woman."

Mitch could be a little hardcore, but Will had recently learned that sometimes the right woman could soften a man up really fast. Bridget made him soft everywhere except his cock. That was pretty much hard any time he was around her. Didn't his sister deserve a man who wanted her so badly? Who would take care of her? "I've seen the way you look at her."

He shook his head. "I may look, but I'm not stupid enough to touch. I've been down that road twice before. I'm not doing it again. No. Laurel will find some young man and then she'll forget she ever had that thought in her head about me. I'm going to turn in. You might be staying, but I have to head back with Ian tomorrow. I'm witnessing Frankie's takeover. I think it will go smoothly after his father is arrested for embezzlement. We have to thank Adam for catching that. Night."

Will watched as his best friend walked away. If Mitch had turned around, he would have caught Laurel watching, too. His sister watched Mitch with longing in her eyes.

But that was drama for another day.

His wife turned and her smile was brighter than the sun. She made her way up the beach to him. "Hello, Doctor Daley."

He kissed her. "Hello, Mrs. Daley. I think we should skip the party and start the honeymoon early." He picked her up, hauling her against his chest. "What do you say?"

"You know I always say yes to you," she replied, putting her arms around his neck.

As the party went on, he snuck his bride away to start their lives together, fully intent on giving his wife the happy ending she deserved.

Author's Note

I'm often asked by generous readers how they can help get the word out about a book they enjoyed. There are so many ways to help an author you like. Leave a review. If your e-reader allows you to lend a book to a friend, please share it. Go to Goodreads and connect with others. Recommend the books you love because stories are meant to be shared. Thank you so much for reading this book and for supporting all the authors you love!

You Only Love Twice
Masters and Mercenaries 8
By Lexi Blake
Coming February 17, 2015

A woman on a mission

Phoebe Graham is a specialist in deep cover espionage, infiltrating the enemy, observing their practices, and when necessary eliminating the threat. Her latest assignment is McKay-Taggart Security Services, staffed with former military and intelligence operatives. They routinely perform clandestine operations all over the world but it isn't until Jesse Murdoch joins the team that her radar starts spinning. Unfortunately so does her head. He's gorgeous and sweet and her instincts tell her to trust him but she's been burned before, so he'll stay where he belongs—squarely in her sights.

A man on the run

Since the moment his Army unit was captured by jihadists, Jesse's life has been a nightmare. Forced to watch as those monsters tortured and killed his friends and the woman he loved, something inside him snapped. When he's finally rescued, everyone has the same question—why did he alone survive? Clouded in accusations and haunted by the faces of those he failed, Jesse struggles in civilian life until McKay-Taggart takes him in. Spending time with Phoebe, the shy and beautiful accountant, makes him feel human for the first time in forever. If someone so innocent and sweet could accept him, maybe he could truly be redeemed.

A love they never expected

When Phoebe receives the order to eliminate Jesse, she must choose between the job she's dedicated her life to and the man who's stolen her heart. Choosing Jesse would mean abandoning everything she believes in, and it might mean sharing his fate because a shadowy killer is dedicated to finishing the job started in Iraq.

* * * *

"Who do you work for?"

"I work for Ian Taggart, though I suspect he's going to fire me."

"Phoebe, I need to know who you work for." Jesse's voice was harder than she'd ever heard before. His jaw had tightened, and when he stood in front of her she could have sworn he grew a couple of inches.

"Phoebe Graham. Accountant. 1266745." She held the bottle, though Aidan's hands came up over hers. She wasn't sure how she could ever thank Li and Avery for these last few moments of sweetness. When this was done and she was back at whatever house she would live in from now on, she wouldn't be the same. If Ten allowed her, she would go back to China and bury herself there. She wouldn't make friends. She wouldn't watch babies. She would do her work and wait to join her husband again.

She wouldn't think about Jesse. She wouldn't remember what it felt like the first time his hand had found hers and for just a minute she'd felt safe again.

"Do you work for Tennessee Smith?" The question dropped from his mouth like a mine just waiting to go off.

Damn, but she always knew he was smarter than anyone gave him credit for. She was fairly certain she didn't react to it at all. "Who is that? Are you talking about that guy who comes in from time to time? The one with the Southern accent? Why would I work for him?"

"Avery, would you please take the baby?" Jesse asked.

Avery stepped up, giving Phoebe a little smile. "Sorry. Li and I should probably move the kiddos. I think Grace is going forward with the party after Charlotte stops yelling at Ian. We're pretty sure the cake won't last so this shower is happening. If you think about it, it's really kind of fitting. Shower and an interrogation. It welcomes Cooper to the family properly."

Li had Carys and Tristan in either arm. He stopped in front of Jesse. "You need some backup?"

Jesse's face was perfectly stony as he shook his head. He didn't even look Li's way, his eyes steady on her.

Pissed. This was what Jesse Murdoch looked like when he was pissed. She'd never seen this side of him. He was usually so casual, so tender and polite with her. When she'd first met him she'd spent months studying him and trying to figure out who the hell he was. She'd envisioned him as hardened and cynical, as though she would be able to see his darkness immediately.

She saw a little of it now. She was shocked to find out it didn't have the effect on her she thought it would have.

Jesse was always sweet, tender. When he looked at her with such softness on his face, she couldn't help but think about Jamie and the way he'd been.

She wasn't thinking about Jamie now. Her body tightened at the way he leaned over, his eyes hard and that sensual mouth of his a flat line. He put both his hands on the table and squared his shoulders.

"What is your mission?"

A simple enough question and she wished she could answer him, but that answer led back to the one question she had to ignore. "To keep McKay-Taggart's books in tip-top shape."

"Do you think I can't handle you, sweetheart?" The words rolled from his mouth, dark and deep and rich.

Was this the man who spent his nights at Sanctum? She knew what happened there. There was no question in her mind when she dismissed him for the night, he went to Sanctum, and she'd come to loathe the place though she'd never been inside. All she could see was Jesse finding the affection and comfort she couldn't provide. She'd closed her eyes more than once and been able to see him making love to another woman, but she'd never really seen him like this. She'd expected he was just as sweet when he made love as he was with her.

What if he was dirty?

"Do you think if you put me off enough I'll walk away and let you be? The time for that is over. It was over the minute you pointed that rifle at my chest. I know I've been following you around like a pathetic moron for months, but that's over, too. It's going to be my way all the way from here on out."

Her heart was thumping in her chest, her body warming. Arousal. At least she remembered what to call it. She'd felt it with him before, but Jamie always hovered between them. When Jesse would reach for her, she would see Jamie's sweet face and back away. Jesse wasn't reaching for her now. He was clearly drawing battle lines, and something about it called to her. A primal energy started to run through her system.

"Your way?" Her voice deepened, her body prepping for battle. This was what she needed. She needed him to see the real her. She needed to test herself against him and find out who was going to come out on top.

"Yes. Mine. I don't suspect you'll like my way so it would be easier to just give me what I want and we can go our separate ways."

She didn't want to go her separate way. That was the whole the problem. The idea of even spending a couple more hours with him tempted her beyond belief. Even if he spent the whole time interrogating her.

She let go of trying to play sweet Phoebe Graham and allowed Phoebe Grant to surface for the first time in a long time.

Phoebe Grant was what Jesse would very likely call a brat. She wondered how Jesse would handle Phoebe Grant. "Bite my ass, sweetheart."

A little thrill went through her spine as his eyes flared, emotion showing for the first time since he'd walked into the room. "Don't say I didn't warn you."

He strode to her, his boots sounding even on the carpet. He scooped her up and tossed her over his shoulder, her ass high in the air.

Phoebe worried she'd bitten off more than she could chew.

Adored: A Masters and Mercenaries Novella
Masters and Mercenaries 8.5
By Lexi Blake
Coming May 12, 2015

A man who gave up on love

Mitch Bradford is an intimidating man. In his professional life, he has a reputation for demolishing his opponents in the courtroom. At the exclusive BDSM club Sanctum, he prefers disciplining pretty submissives with no strings attached. In his line of work, there's no time for a healthy relationship. After a few failed attempts, he knows he's not good for any woman—especially not his best friend's sister.

A woman who always gets what she wants

Laurel Daley knows what she wants, and her sights are set on Mitch. He's smart and sexy, and it doesn't matter that he's a few years older and has a couple of bitter ex-wives. Watching him in action at work and at play, she knows he just needs a little polish to make some woman the perfect lover. She intends to be that woman, but first she has to show him how good it could be.

A killer lurking in the shadows

Assigned to work together on an important case, Mitch and Laurel are confronted with the perfect opportunity to explore their mutual desire. Night after night of being close breaks down Mitch's defenses. The more he sees of Laurel, the more he knows he wants her. Unfortunately, someone else has their eyes on Laurel and they have murder in mind.

Ripper
Hunter, A Thieves Series, Book 1
By Lexi Blake
Coming January 20, 2015

Kelsey Atwood is a private detective with a problem. She came from a family of hunters, growing up on the wrong side of the supernatural world. Tracking down bail jumpers and deadbeat dads may not make her a lot of friends, but it's a lot safer than the life she turned her back on. She was hoping to escape from the nightmares of her past, but her latest case has brought them right back to her door.

A young woman has gone missing, and she didn't go willingly. When Kelsey discovers that the girl is actually a shifter, she knows she should drop the case and walk away. But this shifter was a sweet kid, and she's in serious trouble. More females are missing and the evidence points to a legendary killer. Bodies are piling up, and her case is becoming center stage for a conflict that could shatter the fragile peace between wolves and vampires.

As the hunt intensifies, she finds herself trapped between two men—Gray, a magnetic half-demon lawman, and the ancient vampire Marcus Vorenus. Both men call to her, but when a shocking secret about Kelsey's family is revealed, it could ruin them all. To stop the killer, she will have to embrace the truth about who—and what—she truly is.

* * * *

Gray sat down on the bed again, reaching out to take my hand. I wouldn't give it to him so he settled his palm on my knee. "Have you ever made love, sweetheart?"

It was an utterly ridiculous question and I felt my face heating up. "Don't be ridiculous. I'm not a virgin. I've had sex before."

"With anyone who gave a shit about you?"

Anger replaced the embarrassment because he'd hit the nail on the head and I didn't want to face that fact. I no longer cared if he saw my tits. I pushed his hand off me.

"Fuck you, Gray," I said with every intention of getting out of the house. It didn't matter that it was the middle of the night and I didn't have a car. I would risk it.

His face became a mask of implacable will. As I started to get up, his hand shot out and grabbed my ankle. Before I knew what was happening, his full weight pinned me to the bed and he used his hands to twist something around my wrists. It happened so quickly, I couldn't stop it. My hands were bound tightly together with what looked like black lace.

I stared up at the sight of my hands, too shocked at the moment to be truly pissed off. "Are those my panties?"

"They are indeed, sweetheart." Gray didn't move, continuing to use his two hundred twenty pounds of pure muscle to hold my one twenty down. He leaned slightly to the side, and I heard the nightstand drawer open. His erection was even harder than it had been before, and I hadn't thought that was possible. He twisted his hips to grind against my pelvis and I couldn't stop a little gasp of surprise. That felt really good. "Those are your pretty little panties and these are my handcuffs. Regulation Ranger issue."

He snapped one around the material between my wrists and the other he clipped to the wrought iron in the headboard. He got off the bed and those violet eyes of his stared down at his handiwork.

Naked. I'd been naked before but no one ever made me feel the way Gray did. He studied me like I was a painting he thought fascinating. He'd tied me up so I had no where to run and then he took his time. He caressed me with his stare. The man didn't have to touch me to make my nipples peak or my skin feel alive. And he didn't have to say a damn word to make me vulnerable to him. I was laid out and open, and I was fairly certain that even if he'd untied me, I wouldn't have run. Yeah, that scared me more than I can say.

When he was through with his study, he leaned his big body over and brushed his lips against mine. He didn't attack or try to prove his strength. He did with his mouth what he'd done with his eyes. Slowly and with perfect patience, he explored. I had no way to protest, so I got to do what I had wanted to do in the first place; enjoy the feel of his mouth on mine. I tried to stay in control all the time, tried to direct the world around me, and now I had to wonder why. Just "being" was a foreign concept, but now I relaxed and let myself be with Gray. The man knew how to kiss. After he'd kissed my lips and cheeks and chin and nose, his tongue ran across my mouth, seeking entry. I gave it with a sort of lazy abandon, giving myself over to this moment out of time. His tongue dove deep, twisting around mine like muscular velvet stroking into me. He held my head in both his hands, keeping me still for his plundering. It seemed like forever before he sat back with a satisfied smile, and one hand reached out to tweak my nipple.

"Do you often tie women up?" Of all the things I'd expected him to do, this was not even on the list. I knew I should be fighting, but this slow seduction was a drug invading my system. I liked the feel of my wrists above my head.

A sensual smile spread across his face and his accent deepened when he was aroused. "As often as they'll let me, darlin'. I like it. You look gorgeous like that. Later, I'll tie your legs down. I'll use silk rope so it won't harm your skin, but you also won't be able to move. You'll be open and I'll be able to do anything I want to you. I'll be able to play with every pretty pink part you have, and I will have you screaming for me. You should understand that I'm a man who likes to play with his toys, and you are going to be my sweet little fuck toy the minute I close that bedroom door. I know how strong you are, Kelsey, but you don't have to be in here. You can relax with me. You can know that I will always take care of you. This first time I want your legs around my waist, squeezing me when you come."

Every word came out of his mouth like hot silk covering me, and a warm rush of arousal pulsed through my system. I came alive at the thought of him inside me. God, I lusted for this man. Before Gray, I had just wanted the physical release of sex and the nearest available guy would do, but now there was only Gray. I worried no one else would ever do it for me after him. And I worried that I had no idea how to give him what he wanted. Arousal fled a little as doubt came roaring back. I hadn't made love before. He was right about that. I'd degraded myself because somewhere deep down I thought I deserved it. Gray was offering me something completely different and it terrified me.

"All right, you had your fun, lawman. Untie me." I gave him my tough-girl voice because I needed to put some distance between us.

He laughed. "That's not happening, Kelsey. It's obvious to me you have no idea what you're doing and I aim to teach you."

"Go to hell, Gray." I pulled at the bindings on my wrists. If I was really honest with myself, I didn't try hard.

His eyes went dark and serious. "I'll get there, baby, but I'm not going until you understand a few things." He knelt on the bed and placed his big hand on my belly. I practically quivered at his touch. "I love you,

Kelsey Atwood. I love you and I'm going to fuck you."

"That doesn't sound so loving to me," I commented.

He smiled and leaned over. "Only because you don't know the difference between getting laid and spending hours fucking someone you can't live without. I'm going to love you until you don't remember what your pussy felt like without my cock in it." He trailed his hand down and gently slid his middle finger across my clitoris, parting my labia and delving inside. He sighed. "That's better. When you jumped on me before, you weren't even wet. It's not supposed to hurt. Don't you look at me like that. I'm not judging you. I'm telling you that I'm different from some guy in a bar. I love you. I'll take care of you."

I had two choices. I could fight and he would eventually let me go. Or I could try for once in my lonely life.

I took a deep breath and decided to play things differently. My instinct was to run, to push him away because I already felt too much for him. But I couldn't walk away from Gray and not just because he was really good with bondage. If he broke my heart, at least I'd have loved someone just once.

I nodded.

"Thank you, sweetheart." He stood and moved to the end of the bed. His hands ran up my legs and I sighed because it felt good and warm everywhere he touched me.

I let my head fall back. "You can let me out now. I won't fight you."

He raised my foot up in his hand. "Hell no, Kelsey. I got you where I want you. Like I said, I'd tie your legs to the post too, but I have plans for them. I'll go easy on you tonight, but eventually I intend to introduce you to some…exotic play."

I looked back up. "Just how kinky are you, Grayson Sloane?"

Their Virgin Mistress
Masters of Menage 7
By Shayla Black and Lexi Blake
Coming April 14, 2015

One wild night leads to heartache…

Tori Glen loves her new job as an image consultant for Thurston-Hughes Inc. The trouble is, she's also in love with the three brothers who own it, Oliver, Rory, and Callum. They're handsome, successful, aristocratic, and way out of this small-town Texas girl's league. So she remains a loyal professional—until the night she finds a heartbroken Oliver desperate for someone to love. Tori knows she should resist…but it's so tempting to give in.

And a desperate plan…

Callum and Rory have denied their desire for Tori, hoping she'll heal their older brother, who was so brutalized by his late wife's betrayal. But when Oliver cruelly turns Tori away in the harsh light of day, she tenders her resignation. Rory and Callum realize that to save their brother, they must embrace the unconventional sort of family they've always wanted—with Tori at its center. And it all starts with seducing her…

That could lead to happily ever after—or murder.

Isolated with the brothers at an elegant English country manor, they begin awakening Tori to the most sensual of pleasures. But consumed with regret, Oliver won't be denied the chance to embrace the only woman worth the risk of loving again. What begins as a rivalry veers toward the future they've only dared to dream of. But a stranger is watching and waiting for a chance at revenge. Can the brothers come together to embrace the woman they love and defeat a killer?

About Lexi Blake

Lexi Blake lives in North Texas with her husband, three kids, and the laziest rescue dog in the world. She began writing at a young age, concentrating on plays and journalism. It wasn't until she started writing romance that she found success. She likes to find humor in the strangest places. Lexi believes in happy endings no matter how odd the couple, threesome or foursome may seem. She also writes contemporary Western ménage as Sophie Oak.

Connect with Lexi online:

Facebook: https://www.facebook.com/lexi.blake.39
Twitter: https://twitter.com/authorlexiblake
Pinterest: http://www.pinterest.com/lexiblake39/
Website: http://www.lexiblake.net/

Sign up for Lexi's newsletter at http://www.lexiblake.net/contact.html.

23319897R00115

Made in the USA
Middletown, DE
21 August 2015